I0570446

Those Necessary Thorns

Derrick Pender

Written by Sabrina Childress

Story by Aretha Cephus

For information regarding special discounts for bulk purchases, please http://www.SabrinaChildress.com

0 1 2 3 4 5 6 7 8 9 10

First Edition: December 2015

Printed in the United States of America

ISBN 10: 0996066942
ISBN 13: 978-0-996066-94-5

DEDICATION

Writing this book has been a labor of love and more than an emotional rollercoaster. Therefore, I'd like to dedicate this book to those who have lost loved ones during the commission of my writing. No one can replace another individual. However, we can all gain from memories. To that end: Deborah Jung, Howard Childress, Nina Childress, Kamari Childress, Tyrone Smith and myself for the loss of Katrina Childress; Clarice Mills, Clarence Mills, Sylvia Mills-Echols and Alfred Miller for Grandma Mills and Irene Goldston; Kortney Small for your mother Sylvia A. Bailey Small; Marcelena Ordaz for aunt Cecilia Castillo; Michael Woodson for your grandfather Willie Turner; Sylvia Mills-Echols, Ean Mills and Raymond Echols II for your "Pops" Raymond Echols I; James Martin for your mother Rachel Virginia Martin; Frank Bass for your father; Devan Cassell for your nephew Elijah Lee Cassell; Malcom Davis for your grandfather Jerry Lee McCullough and your friends; Chanel Dixon for your mother Frecilla "Hope" Dixon.

Life is...until it isn't. Cherish it every moment of every day. As always, an enormous thanks to all who are reading this acknowledgment, and will call me later to ask why I didn't mention them. No worries, I'm protecting you. You're welcome!

CONTENTS

ACKNOWLEDGMENTS

*T*hank you, Mrs. Aretha Cephus, for your spirit and your courage! Thank you also for sharing your story with me and now the world!

*N*ow, I 'd like to extend an extra special thank you to Kimberly Wilkins Starks, Sherry Mosely, and Alexcia James for allowing me to pick your medical minds and using your namesakes in this story.

*T*hank you to all of my readers who keep coming back for more! Trust me, although this series is taking a bow, there is more to come from Sabrina Childress.

SYNOPSIS OF BOOKS 1-2

THOSE NECESSARY THORNS: DESIREE ELIZABETH (BOOK 1)

James made a mistake.
Desiree made a decision.
Raymond took interest.
Tina took action.
They all ended up with scars.

Meet Desiree Elizabeth Taylor. Desiree Elizabeth Taylor (Desi) is a sexy, smart, and no-nonsense kind of woman. Some would say she is wholesome -- while others would gladly call her a bitch. After years of living the life of the perfect wife, friend and business savvy know-it-all, Desiree had a secret that would destroy everything she'd worked so hard to achieve.

The cast of characters in her life are starting to unravel and Desiree is losing control fast! Her marriage is on the rocks and her best friend is turning into a spiteful enemy.

What happens when Desiree decides it is better to ask forgiveness than to ask permission?

THOSE NECESSARY THORNS: SEX AND DECADENCE (BOOK 2)

Desiree Elizabeth Taylor and her cast of charismatic characters: James Jones Taylor, Raymond Humphrey, and Tina Harper are back with a vengeance! The erotic drama that consumed Desiree threatens to destroy her life once and for all.

In this heart-pounding adventure, passion rules and obsession reigns as James restores order in his marriage to Desiree and against the man who he blames for putting it all in jeopardy. All of the painful secrets are revealed when love knows no boundaries.

Once a good girl has gone bad, is she gone forever?

PROLOGUE

There was something about his touch. Something in the way he placed his hands on my hips and rested them there... Always my hips, never my waist.

"Where is everybody?"

"What everybody? It's just me and you."

1

*"But worthless men are all like thorns
that are thrown away,
for they cannot be taken with hands"*
2 Samuel 23:6

When I walked into the waiting room of the
plain brown brick building that I'd come to know so
well, I immediately inhaled deeply and exhaled with
relief. Like an old familiar friend the strategically
placed plants, brown cloth couch, brown leather
chairs on either side of the couch and glass coffee
table in the center were all in their respective places.
The receptionist, Nancy, who was seated behind the
tall privacy nook covering most of the desk, greeted
me.

"Hello there Mrs. Taylor. It's a beautiful day
out isn't it?"

"Yes, it is," I smiled wholeheartedly. "I hope I
made this an easy day for you," I winked.

"You most certainly did! Once I get you all
checked in, I can start my weekend a few hours
early," she said with a wide smile.

"Glad I could help."

"You are just the sweetest. Feel free to head
back when you're ready. She's expecting you."

"Thank you. Enjoy your weekend," I said as I soaked in the uncomplicated motif of the space. It made sense if you thought about it; people come to places like this to find simplicity. I can't explain why I loved how much everything here served a purpose. I opened the heavy wooden door next to Nancy's desk which lead to a small corridor and promptly opened the second door on the right. Once inside I was motioned to take a seat; I spoke as I did.

"It's been awhile since I could hold my head up high," I said confidently to the woman who helped me regain my sanity, Dr. Anirbas. "It's been awhile since I could say everything I can't remember, as fucked up as it all may seem," I continued.

It's been a few months since the good doctor and I have been acquainted. Her office has been a safe haven for my emotional wellbeing, and I was very grateful that my best friend, Tara, recommended her services.

It wasn't too long ago that Dr. Anirbas took a deep breath and said, "Recovery is going to take some time, Desi. I think we should start from the beginning. You mentioned a tragedy when you were younger. Tell me about your brother, Derrick Pender."

Truthfully, I still wasn't ready to get into all of that when she made such a proclamation. I was doing my best to process the fact that one of my best friends had betrayed me; I murdered my unborn child; my husband almost fatally shot my lover, and my lover was caught up in a prostitution ring. At that point, my life felt like a Lifetime movie, and I was playing the starring role of the stupid woman who couldn't figure things out. However, the combination of the calming safety of the room and the reassuring sincerity in her eyes softened me enough to open up more than I ever intended. So I decided, today was the day… the day I would tell it all in its entirety; the day I wouldn't hold anything back.

There was a knock on the door, and I reached over to open it without asking who it was. It could only have been one person, my husband James. When I called to make my appointment, I made doubly sure to reserve the entire afternoon. It was going to take that long for me to get all of this out, once and for all. I assured my husband James that I needed to do this, and he should be there.

At first he disagreed and advised me that my sessions should remain private, which I thought was really sweet of him. However I insisted that he be present because I was only going to say these things one time and one time only. I knew there would be questions, and I also knew that there were answers somewhere hiding in all of this mess. Maybe I didn't personally have them, but maybe the three of us could collectively figure it out.

James took a seat on the couch next to me and nodded a hello to Dr. Anirbas. She smiled back, and I asked both of them to take the two seats in front of me. I needed their full attention; I needed to see their eyes. I cleared my throat and poured a glass of water as I sat across from my husband and my therapist. The glass was cold, just what I needed. I adjusted my hips and took a long sip before speaking.

"Please be patient with me today. There is a lot that I need to get off my chest..." As I spoke my eyes prematurely began to well with tears.

"...A lot that you don't know about me." I said looking at James before dropping my eyes to the floor. He shifted uncomfortably in his chair but remained silent.

"Take your time Desiree. We are here for you," Dr. Anirbas said in the familiar nurturing tone that only she could deliver.

"Okay," I said taking another deep breath. "Where should I begin?"

2

My heart had been heavy for far too long. The time had come, and I needed to break free from the things in my past that continually weigh me down. Please bear with me because the truth is stranger than fiction.

I was born Desiree Elizabeth Pender to Rose Thorn and Jacob Pender. My parents weren't married then and, by the time my mother gave birth to me, my father had been drafted into the military. The day I was born my mother handed me to my Momma and disappeared for the duration of my father's five-year tour. I hadn't known any other woman or man to be my parents except Elizabeth and Derrick Thorn, until the age of seven. I know. I know, the math doesn't add up, but it will in a minute.

To this very day everyone says I'm the spitting image of Elizabeth Thorn, from my caramel skin tone, dimples, brown eyes and round face to my shapely body, thick thighs, and full breast. My Momma adored me as I adored her. She was the person who raised me -- my protector, my nurturer, my calm, and my peace. She wasn't quiet, but she was never outspoken either. She always had a calm assertiveness about her that commanded respect in the gentlest way. My Poppa was a stern man who didn't explain himself to anyone for any reason. He was a tall, thin, fairly light brown man with wavy hair who looked of Puerto Rican descent. He was notorious for never smiling, that is until I came along. Strange that even with four kids of their own, he was such a stern man, unless I was around.

In case you haven't figured it out by now, my Momma and Poppa were my biological grand-parents. My mother gave me to my Momma as a gift because my Momma lost her last child before I was born. As odd as it sounds, it was a wonderful arrangement, until my seventh birthday.

It was the morning of my birthday; I awoke to the smell of apple pancakes and bacon wafting through the house. I heard my bedroom door open, and my Poppa creep across the loud wooden floor towards my bed. I pretended to be asleep so he could tickle me awake as he normally did when it was his turn to get me up in the morning. I giggled genuinely as he sang happy birthday to me.

"Thank you Poppa!" I giggled pushing the covers off to the side.

"It's time for breakfast Muffin," he announced. "Get your slippers on and come downstairs. Be sure to speak to Ms. Brown when you go down."

"Yes, sir," I said running to the closet to grab my housecoat and slippers. I followed his giant footsteps down the hallway and onto the stairs. I hopped off of the bottom two steps of the stairwell of our large Victorian house and landed in the middle of the kitchen doorway where my Momma was scooping pancakes from the pan onto a plate and chatting with Mrs. Brown. Every morning Momma had tea with her best friend, Mrs. Brown. Momma stood a good five feet and nine inches tall from the ground up, whereas Mrs. Brown was a smaller five feet and six inches. It always tickled me how much Momma towered over her friend. I was sure that's why Mrs. Brown was so mean; she was always trying to prove herself.

My Momma was my super hero, and her cape was her apron. Momma's apron was nothing fancy to the naked eye, but I knew what each stitch on it meant. She'd made it herself, but she let me pick the thread colors every time she added something to it; I admired that apron. When she put it on it meant that something special was going on, and today that something special was my birthday!

I pranced into the kitchen and took a seat at the round wooden table. She placed a plate in front of me and said, "Happy birthday Muffin! I don't believe I heard you speak to Mrs. Brown."

"Good morning Mrs. Brown," I said dryly.

"Good morning, *little* girl," she answered snidely.

"Good. Now say your grace and drink your milk half way before you touch a pancake," Momma said sweetly.

"Yes, ma'am!" I said smiling from ear to ear. I rushed through a standard, "*God is great. God is good. Let us thank HIM for our food. Amen*" prayer and swallowed as much milk in one gulp as I could before digging into the sweet and savory apple, bacon, and caramel compote that was drizzled on my pancakes. I loved those pancakes better than any dessert, and she knew it!

"Alright, Derrick, take a seat," she ordered him. "We've got a big day ahead of us. The family will be over in a few hours, and I've got to get this house straightened up."

"Derrick, are you going to join us this morning?" Mrs. Brown asked flirtatiously, getting up from her seat preparing to leave.

"Nope," he responded quickly to Mrs. Brown before taking his seat while turning his attention to Momma with a slightly annoyed tone.

"I know Elizabeth... can't we just take our time?" he said looking over at me. "It's not every day someone turns the big seven."

I loved the way he said my age. He always made it seem like a really big number, as if I were almost as adult as him and he couldn't believe it. It was always so very special. My Momma looked at us and smiled as she wiped her hands on a towel and laid it on the counter top.

"I'm going to sit down for a few minutes. Come and get me when the dishes are done."

"Okay," I answered quickly. Poppa and I ate our breakfast in silence. Once we'd finished, he set up the stool next to the sink so I could reach the counter. He washed the dishes and I dried them. He put them away and took a look around before we walked out of the kitchen down the hall towards their bedroom where Momma had gone to rest. When we walked into the room, my heart started pounding as Poppa sat on the bed and poked at Momma. My eyes welled with tears and I could hear him saying, "Elizabeth. Elizabeth. Wake up baby. Elizabeth…"

She didn't move. My body stiffened as I stared at the blank expression on my Momma's face. Her eyes were open, and they were filled with nothing but the blacks of her eyes and space. They were looking right at me.

I could tell she wasn't there anymore. I knew she wasn't in her body anymore. I can't explain it but although I couldn't move, my brain told me that my Momma was gone, but she was still with me. That was the first time that the Earth stood still in my life… the day I realized eyes truly are the soul. She'd laid across the bed and died...on my birthday no less!

I remember my Poppa yelling at me to go get some help, but I couldn't move. I just couldn't take my eyes off of Momma's. It's like they were calling out to me in some strange spiritual way. He ran past me, out of the front door, and across the street to Mrs. Brown's. They came bursting back into the room, and she took one look and said, "Derrick she's dead."

"She can't be dead Pam! She was just making breakfast!" he shouted back at her.

"I'll call someone," Pam Brown said calmly.

"Poppa..." was all I could say.

"Come on Muffin. You don't need to see this," he said picking up my stiff-as-a-board body and carrying me into the living room.

As we exited the room, I watched her eyes the entire time. He placed me on a chair in the living room and rushed back to the bedroom. I could hear

Mrs. Brown on the phone telling someone we needed help. I remember thinking she would know if someone was dead or not. I'd overheard my Momma telling my aunt that Mrs. Brown had buried two husbands and she shouldn't be looking for a third because she was a black widow.

My trance was broken when I heard the sobs of my Poppa coming from down the hall. I got up from the chair, ran back into the room, and began to cry. The strong man in front of me was holding the stiff body of my Momma in his arms. He was rocking her and rubbing her arms in a failed attempt to warm her back to life.

Before I knew it, I was whisked away once more by the strong arms of my Poppa's brother, who'd arrived at the party early to help move some furniture. I don't remember much after that. I don't remember the funeral or the burial or much of anything else.

Poppa decided that I should live with my great grandmother. My first day as a tenant in her house she told me that I would only be staying until my mother decided to come and get me. Puzzled, I asked her, "Grams are you feeling okay?"

"Yes. Why do you ask?"

"You said I'm staying with you until my Momma comes to get me. Don't you know Momma died; she's in heaven looking down on us now?" I said, somberly reminding her of Momma's death.

"Oh, *chil'* I'm not talking about your *grand*-mother… I'm talking about your *real* mother."

I shook my head in disappointment, "It's okay Grams. I think you might need a nap."

She chuckled at me and her voice became very serious. "Desiree, your *real* mother is your Momma's daughter. I'm your great grandmother. Elizabeth is,.." she paused and swallowed hard before speaking again, "*was* your grandmother, and Rose is your real mother. Rose is Elizabeth's daughter."

She paused once more to observe my reaction.

"Who is Rose?" I asked confused.

"You've never met her. She is coming back here soon to take you back."

"No," I said matter-of-factly. I didn't know that woman. I begged that they didn't let me go with her. I didn't have a say-so in the matter.

Rose Thorn showed up one whole month after her own mother's funeral -- which she'd missed because no one could find her -- and claimed me as her child. Three weeks after that, a man showed up at the door with a five-year-old little boy named Michael Paul Pender, claiming to be my father.

Apparently, my mother got pregnant with another child by my father when he was home on leave. After she gave birth to a baby boy, she dropped him off at my father's sister and disappeared. The four of us moved into the neighboring town and started life as if nothing had ever happened.

3

My special place, the elevated and oversized yellow Victorian house, rested nicely between the first and the third houses from the corner. The front porch was encased behind a white wooden railing that needed a good touch-up job. The rolling green grass of the front yard rested beautifully on a large mound of land. It was spacious enough for a rose garden on one side that housed a small white cast iron seating set for two and a colorful flower garden to the other side.

The two sets of three concrete steps leading up to the stairs of the front porch, spilled onto either side at the base of the wooden stairs. Our backyard was sweeping and very large in size. A weeping willow tree had a standard tire swing attached to one of its branches, which I used as often as I could.

I grew up in a loving home, for the most part, although I cried for my Momma, Elizabeth, most nights. My brother and I had some fun times and we quickly became really close. As the older sister, I felt it was my job to be overprotective.

It was only two and half months after we'd moved when all the drama began; my Poppa who I now know was my grandfather, married my grandmother's best friend in the living room of my old house; she moved right in and banished my birth mother and her sisters from the house after she moved her two kids in. Rumors started to swirl that people suspected her of somehow killing her own husband and my Momma.

To make matters worse, the whole town was spreading nasty lies that her son belonged to my Poppa and not her dead husband.

The family fell apart. People chose sides and a war of words began. No one spoke to each other anymore.

I awoke one morning to my parents arguing loudly in their bedroom. I checked my brother's room to make sure he was ok before tip-toeing my way down the hall to their bedroom. I could hear my mother screaming that my father was a son-of-a-bitch and that she hated him. She hurled insults that would make a sailor blush before he responded in the most calm voice he could muster. "You need to calm down. Don't put this on me, Rosie."

"Fuck you!" she yelled. Then I heard a loud crash. "And don't call me Rosie! I hate that shit!"

"Don't you throw another thing girl!" My father said forcefully.

"Don't you ever tell me what to do…" The vibrations in her voice shook my soul they were so deep.

"I'll be back when you calm down," Jacob informed Rose.

The door swung open and I stood there wide-eyed and frozen. He looked at me and his angrily hard face softened. He picked me up and kissed my cheek, "Hey baby girl. You know you shouldn't be listenin' to grown folks' talk like that."

"I'm sorry," I said squeezing his wide neck.

"I'm sorry too. I hope we didn't scare you," he replied trying to reassure me, but before I could speak, my mother pried my hands from around him and yanked my out of his arms. I fell to the floor, and she didn't even look at me.

"Leave!" She shouted staring into his face. Without another word, my father walked out of the door. My mother turned on her heels and stomped back into the bedroom where she promptly slammed the door.

I sat on the floor and cried as only a seven-year-old could. My nose ran and my eyes burned. After a few minutes, I went into my brother's room, climbed into his bed and hugged him tight, then fell asleep.

I'm not sure how long we slept, but it couldn't have been long before my mother burst open the door and yelled, "Put some clothes in a bag!" Michael and I both jumped out of our skin. I moved quickly, grabbing one small duffle bag and a suitcase and put all of the clothes I could manage into them. Rose yelled from the front of the house for us to come outside. Still dressed in our pajama's and slippers, I handed the smaller bag to my brother and tugged him by the hand.

"Where are we going Desi?" he asked sleepily.

"I don't know Michael. Rose just wants us to come outside."

"Momma, not Rose..." he scolded me. I'd gotten in trouble a few times since meeting Rose, for calling her by her first name instead of Momma as she demanded.

"Whatever," I said still tugging at him.

Once we made it to the front porch, she was already in the car waiting. I figured she was going to take us to where Daddy was. I knew it upset her when I called Jacob *Daddy* and her Rose, but I didn't care. Jacob was warm and caring and friendly, whereas she was hot and cold and generally demanding most of the time. She was always upset about something. Her beautiful face was hard to see under the scowl that she wore every day.

I opened the back door of the car and ushered my brother in before pushing the bags on the floor and climbing in myself.

"Are you taking us to Daddy?" I asked stiffly. Before I could blink, I felt a sting on my round cheeks that radiated throughout my face. I instinctively grabbed my face as tears welled up in my eyes.

The back of her hand was still in the air as she spoke, "Call him daddy one more time!" She snapped peering at me through dark eyes. I sat still and willed myself not to let a tear drop from my eyes. I was not going to give her the satisfaction. She turned in the seat and jerked the car out of the driveway.

We must have driven for about two hours before the car came to a stop in front of a house in much need of tender love and care. There was a very tall man sitting on the porch drinking a beer. He stood to address her, as Rose opened the driver's side door.

"Well, well, look what the cat drug in, Rose

Thorn!"

"Hey, Ron!" She said with a smile too big for anyone who'd just slapped the taste out of a seven-year-old's mouth.

"How are you? It has been a long time," she continued flirtatiously.

I watched through the window as the pair met in the middle of the sidewalk and hugged tightly until a woman appeared at the door. They quickly disengaged and stepped back from one another.

"Hey, Arlene," Rose said looking into the screen door.

"Hey, Rosie," Arlene said dryly. "What are you doing here?"

"Guess I'll get right to it then," Rose said as she approached the door of the house and Ron followed. They were in the house for over an hour while Michael and I sat in the hot car. He'd gone back to sleep, but I was watching the door like a hawk.

Finally, Rose emerged and yelled from the front porch, "Desiree! Michael! Come in here!" I shook Michael awake and we scooted out of the backseat. Once we made it to where she stood, she told us to go in and say hello to our aunt Arlene. We did as we were told.

When we walked into the house, our noses were assaulted with an odor of spoiled fish and dirty socks. The white walls were smeared with fingerprints and dirt; there was a pile of clothes in the corner of the living room. From where I stood, I could see into the kitchen where a pile of dirty dishes were stacked up and overflowing out of the sink. I could tell they'd been there for awhile because flies were circling the area.

"Hi, Aunt Arlene," we said in unison.

"Hi," she said looking us up and down.

"Look at the dimples on these two," Ron said pinching our cheeks.

"Well, don't just stand there. Have a seat."

"Yes, ma'am," I responded for the both of us as I tugged my brother for the second time that day.

"Your cousins will be here in a minute. Just sit there and wait," she said with the same disgruntled look that my mother always had. We inched our way over to a couch that was badly stained and appeared wet in at least one spot.

We sat closely to each other quietly for a half an hour before I finally asked, "When will Rose be back?"

"Stay out of grown folks' business," was her response.

Another thirty minutes had gone by before three not-so-kept kids came bounding in the door. They came rushing over to us, asked our names and how long we'd be staying with them. Puzzled, I went to the front porch and found our bags resting there.

Our mother had left my brother and me with a complete stranger. Aunt or not I was tired of meeting my family members this way; however my aunt thought it was hilarious. She called us Rose's little mistakes…those were the hardest three years. Aunt Arlene was worse than Rose.

For three long years, I was made to wash everyone's clothes, clean the house, do the dishes, and sometimes cook meals. I was whipped almost every single day and during school months, I was given five minutes to get home or else.

Arlene was just mean, and I could never understand why. I couldn't understand why my mother left us like that.

4

It's funny how people say GOD works in mysterious ways. I mean laughable funny! What kind of GOD puts two innocent children right smack in the middle of a living hell for no good reason?! You tell me?

I was in sixth grade and enslaved to her for allowing me and my brother to live under her roof in one filthy bedroom with her three kids. Every time I cleaned it up, they'd mess it up. If her kids were bad, I got a whipping with this thick blue water hose.

In the two months before Rose decided to show up in my life again, I'd had it! I was completely done with life at the age of eleven. I remember dreading going home every single day and even worse her five-minute rule. It was damn near impossible to do every day.

One day I couldn't get across the train; it was moving too fast. My classmate ran to my house to tell my aunt Arlene that I couldn't get across. She could care less. "She said you better get across!" he reported over the loud freight train.

When I made it home, she screamed every profanity and ugly name she could think of at me.

This was nothing new. I'd almost perfected

tuning her out completely. She was always verbally abusive to me and my brother, but not to her own children. When she noticed I wasn't listening to her rant any longer, she became violent. She grabbed my throat and began to squeeze tightly. I scratched and clawed at her manly hands until she released me.

Aunt Arlene had increasingly inflicted physical pain on me until she was satisfied. As I stood there holding my throat and trying to regain my breath, she reentered the room with a thick blue water hose. Instead of folding it over like a belt as she usually did, she swung it wildly at me as I tried to dodge its sting. She landed one. I screamed in pain. She landed another. I screamed again. I was screaming so loudly that I was sure Jesus heard me all the way in heaven.

Tonight is the night she is going to actually kill me. Although I was in more pain than I'd ever felt in my life, but I wasn't afraid. A blow landed on my right temple and my small, frail frame fell to the floor. My vision was blurry, and I could just barely see her feet shuffle out of the room. I thought it was the ringing in my head, but it wasn't. It was the doorbell.

I heard the door open and a police officer identify himself, "Is everything all right here?" he asked assertively.

"Yes, everything is fine. Why do you ask officer?"

"We received a report that someone's in trouble at this address," he said.

"No. Not here," she said with a half smile. "Just

the kids probably being too rough with each other."
I lay on the floor sincerely thanking Jesus for
hearing me. Someone finally called the police
because I was crying so loud. I knew that if I got off
the floor and went into the front of the house, they
would be able to tell that something was wrong.
They would rescue me and Michael, and we would
be okay.

The possibility of being saved allowed me to
muster up enough strength to stumble into the
always filthy living room. When the officer saw me,
he moved past my aunt and asked, "Are you okay
young lady?"

"Yes, she's fine. Like I said, you know how
these kids are. I just told them about playing too
rough," Arlene answered quickly stepping in front
of me.

"I was asking the girl ma'am," he said moving
her aside.

"Everything is fine officer," Ron said entering
the house. The officer turned to face him as he
continued. "I'm here now and as my wife told you,
these kids can be a handful," he said glancing at me.
"It won't happen again. We will keep it down from
now on."

"Alright, make sure you do. If we get another
call, we're gonna know something," the officer
warned. "I wouldn't expect anything less," Ron
replied ushering the officer toward the door.

I couldn't speak. The words wouldn't come out.
I stood there wondering why he couldn't see that
something was wrong here. Once that door closed,
it was at that moment I knew, for sure, there was

nothing *anyone* could do for us. *There was no help.*
If we were going to get out of here, I would have to
do it myself... then I fainted.

When I came to, my brother informed me that
I'd been out for a full day and a half. Michael ran
through the house announcing that I'd woken up. I
glanced around the room and focused on the
roaches crawling out of a pile of clothes in the
corner in an attempt to steady my vision, when I
heard Aunt Arlene yelling that she was going to
whoop my brother; I came out to his rescue.

She accused Michael of smearing the already
disgusting walls with a dirty hand. Anyone with
half a brain could see that the print was too big to be
Michael's. It was clearly her son's handprint on the
wall. I couldn't and wouldn't allow her to abuse my
brother like she'd done to me for the past three
years. It was *her* son that did that to the wall. I
wasn't being protected, but I wanted to be his
protector.

Although I wasn't allowed to talk back to adults
I came barreling out of the bedroom and shouted, "I
did the damn shit!"

"What did you say?!" Aunt Arlene said turning
in my direction. "Go get a switch!" she ordered
Ron. He immediately left the house, and when he
returned, he brought in a tree branch. He dropped
the oversized piece of wood at Aunt Arlene's feet. I
was confused. *Why would he bring a whole tree
branch? Maybe the bump on my head had
permanently altered my ability to gauge size.*

He looked at Arlene then over at me, and then
to Michael and Arlene's son. A sly grin crept across

his face. Suddenly, everyone started laughing.

I looked around the room more confused than ever. For some reason unknown to myself, I joined in with an awkward, uncomfortable laugh. It dawned on me that Ron was trying to help the situation. It was odd, but it worked. That was the first time we'd all actually laughed together.

Nobody got a whipping that day. My uncle was always really nice, but my aunt was just a hot mess.

The following week, Arlene was back at her old tricks, but she'd wait until Ron was not around. She demanded that I do all of the laundry in the house, by hand, in the bathroom tub.

Without one word of objection, I accepted my sentence and entered her bedroom first with a basket in tow. I proceeded to sort the cloths by color as I normally did. When I picked up a pair of pants, a letter drifted from its folds. I picked it up and read:

Dear Desiree and Michael,

I love you guys! I'm glad to hear you are enjoying your time with your aunt. Every time I call she says you're out having fun or sleep or busy. I hope the money I'm sending is helping. Here's the $250.00 as promised. I will be home soon to get you.

I miss and love you both.

Love,

Mom

Two hundred and fifty dollars! That was a lot of money for that time, moreover my brother and I weren't seeing a dime of it. I had small hand-me-downs, everything from my shirt to my shoes!

Aunt Arlene even gave the clothes I came here with to her daughter one week after had we arrived. When I asked for them back, she slapped me in my mouth, and asked me if was I calling her a liar? I would stitch clothes together more times than I could count. *That lying bitch!*

I never told Michael that Rose didn't care because I didn't want him to lose hope. I'm glad I didn't because the letter proved she did care the entire time.

Everything started to make sense! I recalled the goodies Aunt Arlene would flaunt in front of us -- she would buy trinkets, records, cars, hosted lavish parties; her kids got everything.

She never helped us with homework, never took us to the doctor, paid school fee. She wouldn't even comb our hair or take care of us the way she should've. She didn't spend a dime of my mother's child support on us. There I was cutting the back of my gym shoes off and making them into flip flops, and she was stealing from me and my brother. I couldn't wait to tell my brother that our mother did care and actually mean it.

That night was Christmas Eve and all five kids were shuffled off to the bedroom for bedtime. Aunt Arlene's oldest son didn't realize that the puppy had burrowed into the mattress. He sat on him and instantly killed the dog; I had to clean it up.

As I picked up the dead carcass and scrubbed

the blood, guts and slime from the hole in the mattress, I decided that I was going to go find my mother.

I told Michael of my plan and made him stay in bed after promising that I'd return with Rose. I waited until it was dark out and everyone had gone to bed. I tiptoed into the bathroom and jumped out of the bathroom window.

I didn't know where I was going or how I was going to find Rose. I walked for over an hour before coming upon a social club. The night air howled; it was dark, and I had no idea where I was going. The cold air was starting to change the color of my lips, when my grandmother's voice whispered, "Go back home."

I looked around for any resemblance of her, and I started to cry. I wasn't sure if it was a combination of the cold and the concussion I'd had, but I took off running. When I got back to the house I went through the very window I'd climbed out of and found my brother; he was crying and scared.

"Did you find her Desi?" he whimpered.

"No. Not yet… But we will," I assured him.

"I called her."

"You called her?" I questioned.

"Yeah. The lady operator said she'd find her and tell her that I called."

"Go to sleep Michael."

"Good night. I love you."

"I love you too. Good night," I said kissing his temple.

Christmas morning came. The stillness of the house was no different than any other day. Michael and I didn't look forward to this day like Aunt Arlene's kids did. We never got anything. Being good or bad that year didn't make any difference to "Santa Claus" because we were the forgotten two.

Every single gift under the tree would be for their family, and we'd have to sit and watch as they all opened the many beautiful boxes and trinkets left for each of them. We were told year after year that, "Your mother didn't bother to send you anything. She must be busy."

That memory would replay in my mind over and over again, as I stirred under the pressure of Michael's head on my arm. My three cousins had already gone to the front of the house to see what goodies awaited them. I could hear the tearing of paper and *oooh's* and *aaaah's* echoing throughout the house. I listened for a minute or two then placed my hands over my ears so I couldn't hear anymore when the doorbell rang.

I took my hands off of my ears and shifted my body so I could sit up and hear who was visiting so early in the morning. Secretly I was hoping it was the officer coming to check on us this Christmas morning. If it was, I was going to run down the hall and tell him everything and beg him to take me and my brother with him. Now that would be a sight to see and some much-needed embarrassment for Aunt Arlene.

I giggled before coming out of my thoughts and recognized one of the voices coming from the front of the house. It was my Poppa's voice! The next voices I heard was my daddy's and then Rose's!

"Michael! Michael!" I shouted shaking him

wildly! "Get up! Rose is here! Poppa is here! They came to save us!" I was so excited, I nearly tossed him out of bed trying to get up.

I ran down the hall to the kitchen where the voices were wafting and slid into the first adult lap I recognized. My Poppa hugged me tight and picked me up.

"There's my Muffin!" he said squeezing me again. "Let me take a look at you."

I hopped down and hugged his waist again, "I'm so happy to see you! Merry Christmas!" I squeaked and instantly removed the smile from my face when I noticed the look on his. I stepped back and surveyed the room. I looked at my Poppa, then Daddy, and finally at Rose.

Their faces were of disapproval. I felt shamed, naked and very scared at the same time. I stood there for what felt like an hour, allowing their eyes to probe me inch by inch until Rose decided to speak first.

"Why does my child look like a ragamuffin?" she asked, turning toward Aunt Arlene.

"Momma!" Michael's voice shouted as he ran into Rose's arms.

"Michael!" she said disgusted at his appearance. His hair was dirty and needed a good combing and cut. His teeth were stained, and he had crust from sleep down his face.

"What the hell is going on in here?!" Daddy demanded.

"They just haven't had time to clean up. It's early and you know how children are," Arlene said nervously.

"Y'all go get your things," Rose instructed. "We're taking you home." We ran down into the bedroom and found two brown paper bags lying about and threw our clothes into them. I stopped to hug my brother and thank him for calling whoever he called. I wish I would have thought about that sooner! Apparently, when my brother called for my mother he got an operator who contacted the Red Cross, who found my Poppa. He called my daddy, and he called Rose.

It sounds strange, but I really think my Momma had whispered in my ear last night. I really believe my Momma's spirit had come to save me. It was really her! No lie. It didn't matter now; the people who loved us came to find us.

I could hear my daddy scolding my mother for leaving us with "that trifling bitch". Then I heard the front door slam and Ron tell my Poppa, "You better watch your mouth. The only trifling bitch 'round here is Rose."

As we walked back into the kitchen, Rose was sitting at the table talking to my aunt. She said something about a buddy system and joining the military before she stopped speaking in mid-sentence, when she saw that we only had two brown bags. "Didn't I tell you two to go get *all* of your things?"

"Yes, ma'am we did. This is all of our stuff."

My Poppa, who'd been sitting on the stained couch next to the front door stood to approach us; I would swear I saw a tear in his eye. The next thing I knew, I grabbed my brother from harm's way and my Poppa ushered us out the door because my mother had jumped up from the table and snatched Arlene by her collar; she went ballistic! She yelled something about her checkbook, tacky kids, and fucking Ron.

My mother beat my aunt's ass from one end of the house to the other! Once we were outside, my Poppa and daddy got us safely into the car, and they ran back into the house after Ron to break up the fight. I'm certain my daddy didn't hear that crack about Rose fucking Ron, but I sure did! I vowed then and there, never ever to be like Rose Thorn.

My mother took us home, to another new house, in a new neighborhood about twenty minutes from my Poppa and his wife Pam and ten minutes from her other sister, my aunt, Angel Thorn. Even though she came, I was still angry.

5

The next five years of my life were uneventful as compared to those between ages seven and eleven. When Rose "rescued" us from the hell that was Aunt Arlene's, she moved us and her new boyfriend, Lloyd into the new place.

My daddy's face was the saddest I'd ever seen it, even worse than the day he'd left when we pulled up to the new house. He helped us get settled and promised to come visit us every day after work. He kept his promise and that made Michael and I feel safe.

Rose and I were still at odds, and I made sure to give her hell at every turn. My mouth didn't hold any punches and whenever I thought I could get away with it, I would purposefully be disrespectful in front of my daddy. He would scold me and remind me to mind my manners. I'd always agree until the next time. Rose knew that Jacob would have her head if she ever mistreated me in front of him.

On my sixteenth birthday, Jacob and Lloyd both gave me table rings -- a ring you give to your daughter when they turn sixteen. I thanked them both, but kept my daddy's ring on my finger and put Lloyd's away in a safe place.

As I prepared for my first real birthday party, random tears slide down my cheeks like pebbles as I thought about the last *real* birthday party I was supposed to have -- the day my Momma, Elizabeth passed away.

I couldn't help but wonder if this birthday would be just as cursed as that one, considering no one really celebrated my birthday because we always mourned it as the day Momma Elizabeth died.

Every year since we'd moved into the new house, family and friends would gather and have cake and talk about her, and the suspicious circumstances of her death. Pam would be sitting right in their faces and they'd whisper and scowl and ask her how she did it or if she felt like she was going to go to heaven or hell for being a murderous bitch.

Sometimes, they'd even ask her what she was going to do if she ever decided she was done with Poppa. I hated having to sit through these conversations and accusations. My train of thought was broken when I jumped at the sound of the deep voice coming from the doorway of my bedroom.

"Why are you always so mean?" Lloyd asked.

"I'm not mean. You do know you're not my dad, right?"

"Yes, I do know that..." He paused.

"And I don't want you to be," I interjected before he could continue.

"If you just give me a chance, I would be the best stepfather you ever had."

"I just told you, I don't want another new

father, step or otherwise," I said with a grimacing smile.

Honestly, when Rose's boyfriend came into the picture, he kept trying to be our friend. I didn't like him, although he was nothing but nice. He didn't do anything wrong to me, but I just didn't want to be bothered. Not to mention, as long as my mother believed that I hated him, she couldn't accuse me of being fast or eyeing him, as she frequently did when any man came around.

"Well, you better get used to it Desiree Elizabeth, because he's not going anywhere," a pregnant Rose said side stepping into my room.

"Whatever you say, Rose," I said snidely.

"Watch your tone *little* girl." That phrase made me cringe; she sounded just like Pam.

The older I got, the more outspoken I became. I challenged her a lot, and I wasn't scared of anything. I'd turn to look her directly in the eyes and smile. I knew she hated when I did that because she could never figure out what I was thinking or going to do next.

It was my sixteenth birthday, and my mother decided this was the day she'd become every bit of the devil I knew her to be. She took a step closer as if to challenge me to a fight, and I was ready. The only problem was that I couldn't figure out how to dismember her properly without hurting the innocent baby baking in her belly. Before the battle could begin, Lloyd stepped in and directed my mother into the kitchen, but not before turning to apologize for her behavior. This did not sit well with Rose, not one bit.

My guests started to arrive, and I went about being a gracious host. The music was playing and my decorations were a pretty red and purple strewn about the house and the backyard.

I was overjoyed when my daddy arrived with his sisters and their children. I got along great with my father's sisters and their children; they always treated me kindly, like family is supposed to. They joined some other teenagers in the backyard, and I went into my room to grab a hair pin. When I turned around, there was my Lloyd again.

"What now Lloyd? I've got a party to tend to."

"Your mother sent me in here."

"For what?" I asked actually curious.

"She accused you of smoking dope and she said I have to give you a whoopin'," he said in a low voice. I looked down at his left hand and he was holding a belt. The man that just questioned me about why was I so mean and asked to be my stepfather is now standing in my doorway telling me that Rose instructed him to hit me. I didn't understand, and I guess the confused look on my face said just that.

"Listen, I don't want to do this, but she told me if I didn't..." he started to cry.

"Lloyd, I didn't do anything wrong, and I damn sure didn't smoke any dope!"

"But -" he tried to continue.

"If you think for one second that I'm going to let you hit me, you have another thing coming," I said in the most even voice I could muster with all of the anger bubbling inside me.

"I don't want to fight you, but I will." He raised

his hand to hit me and I grabbed the belt; he looked at me and started to cry. He left my room. The next thing I knew, my mother pulled him back into the room and they argued right there in front of me.

"I'm gonna beat your ass!" She shouted.

"Rose, I'm going to tell you once. If you touch me, one of us will not leave this room alive."

Her nostrils were wide and flared, and she was breathing like a dragon; our eyes locked.

She walked out of the room. "For the next week don't you leave this house, listen to a radio, watch a TV or have any company!" she shouted as she exited.

I flopped down on my bed and screamed into a pillow when I heard another voice approaching,

"You ok baby girl?" Jacob asked rubbing my back.

"No! I hate this place and I hate her!"

"You don't hate your mother."

"Yes, I do! Why can't I come live with you?"

"Because a woman should raise a young lady," he replied.

"Do you know what she just did?! She just accused me of smoking dope at my own party and sent Lloyd in here to whoop me," I explained as the tears flowed from my eyes.

"She did what?!" Jacob's face didn't bare the same expressive tone that his statement did.

"Where is he?! Where is she?! I'll kill them both!" he said angrily. "You wait right here," he firmly instructed.

My daddy walked right up to Lloyd and pushed him. Lloyd staggered backwards and began apologizing. My mother came running up behind my daddy, and my father's sister pulled her back by her hair and yanked her down. Rose began shouting nonsense about how I was being fast. She said she didn't trust me and that I was dating Lloyd! Everyone in the place stopped.

"What the *hell* is wrong with you Rose?! That is your own daughter you're talking about!" Lloyd shouted.

"You're a really sick bitch! You know that!" my father added. "You don't want to talk about anybody being fast Rosie! Do you even know whose baby that really is?"

"Y'all don't know what you're talking about! I live with her, and I see how she looks at him."

"I cannot do this anymore!" Lloyd said exiting the scene.

"You are the worst mother in the world," I heard someone say.

Rose ran after Lloyd and they continued to argue. He packed his things and left along with the flow of all of my other partygoers. He kept mumbling how he couldn't take it anymore.

My daddy and aunt came to comfort me as my mother incoherently rambled on about raising kids and how no one understands. Michael said he was going to stay with Daddy because Rose wasn't right in the head; Jacob took him.

Lloyd never came back. My mother had the baby, and my parents got back together after Kenneth was born. There were a lot of arguments and ups and downs in our house because Jacob refused to marry Rose. She accused him of ruining her chances of anyone making an 'honest women' out of her; that in itself was laughable.

Even though she was my birth mother and I learned to love her, I loathed her more and more. Oddly enough, I think Jacob felt the same as I did; for some reason my father loved Rose's dirty panties and, to my knowledge, never cheated on her. I just couldn't understand what he saw in her; she was evil, pure and simple, and a horrible person too. One thing I knew for sure, he wanted us to be a real family, but something was holding him back.

Rose began deliberately doing things to make my daddy's life miserable. For example, she went out and bought a car when his car died and wouldn't let him use it to get to work. She actually made him walk, rain or shine, it didn't matter. She would hit him and then apologize and hit him again while she apologized; he never hit her back.

She'd even told him once that Michael wasn't his son. Although she took it back, my daddy told her he would never forgive her for that; he never treated Michael or Kenneth for that matter, any different.

Then one day, miracle of all miracles, my mother called a family meeting.

"I need everyone at the kitchen table!" She hollered through the house.

"What's this about Rosie?" Jacob asked.

"I'll tell you when everyone is sitting down," she said with a big smile.

"Why are you so happy?" I asked as I entered the kitchen with Kenneth in my arms and Michael at my heels.

"I think it's time things change around here," she said looking at each of us. "I really want this family to be better than mine was. And since we will soon have a new addition, I think it's time we get some things in order because it's getting crowded around here."

My father shifted his eyes from Rose's face to her belly and back again, "Are you saying you're pregnant again?"

"Yes!"

"Oh my God! What are we going to do with another kid around here?!" Michael's reaction surprised everyone. My mother's smile turned into an immediate reprimanding scowl and was immediately removed when my father told her, "Fix your face, Rose! The boy was only saying what we were all thinking. We don't need another mouth to feed around here."

I sat quietly watching the exchange among my family members before I finally spoke, "So, another baby," I said bouncing Kenneth on my lap.

"Yes, Desi, another baby, which means you need to start getting ready to leave this house."

"*Shut up* Rose!" My father said sharply.

"Is there a problem Jacob?"

"Is *this* one mine?" He retorted.

"Don't try me!" she said hitting the counter top with her fist.

"That doesn't answer the question."

"Yes."

"Are you sure?"

"*Are you?*"

"*Hell no*, that's why I asked."

48

"Well, if I were your *wife* you wouldn't have to ask me questions like that."

"If you acted like wife material you would already *be* a wife," Jacob said matter-of-factly. His tone stiffened me, and I started to gather the kids and leave the room.

My mother was pregnant again, and my daddy was not happy. For a moment, I was honestly confused about why my daddy questioned the paternity of the baby Rose was carrying, considering I'd heard them have sex more often than I'd ever like to admit. If he didn't trust her or didn't want another baby, why not stop having sex with her? I was only a teen, but even I could understand that concept.

I knew where this was headed, and I didn't want either of my brothers to remember the beginning of the end.

Jacob decided to move out and go stay at his sister's house nearby. Every morning that we woke he was there, and every night before we went to bed he was there; he just didn't sleep at our address. The months flew by and the house was always filled with awkwardness between my parents.

The ninth month of Rose's pregnancy, Jacob moved back home until she was able to get on her feet. I thought they'd worked it out and things would return to normal. Then all hell broke loose!

I walked into the house just in time to dodge a flying plate that hit the wall, crashed, and shattered.

"Who do you think you are?!" she screamed as she picked up another plate.

"You're crazy!" He shouted back.

"Get out! Get out! Get out! Don't you ever step foot back in this house again!"

"That's a promise I intend to keep," He said picking up a bag he'd apparently packed at some point before I arrived. Jacob stormed passed me as he left our house once again. I don't even think he ever really saw me standing there. The red rage in his eyes pricked my soul. I shook from the chill that ran through me when he passed by.

I asked Rose why she put him out again. She responded, "Stay in a child's place or get the fuck out!"

Our small town swelled with more rumors, no doubt started by the devil known as Rose Thorn that my daddy had hit her, but we knew that wasn't true.

6

The wheels of an old pea green Chevy Impala screeched to a halt in front of the hospital emergency room doors. The passenger door flung open and an unshaven Jacob emerged from the car almost tripping over his own feet. This was going to be the first time he was actually present to witness one of his children entering the world. Unfortunately, this joyous occasion was overshadowed by resentment toward the woman he'd loved so deeply.

The Labor and Delivery department at the local hospital was full, and Jacob ran from room to room looking for Rose. He was slightly agitated that he'd got a call from our neighbor who overheard me and my mother screaming that the baby was coming. He rushed to the hospital only to find that we were not there.

Derrick Thomas Pender was born in the early morning hours of an exceptionally chilly November day, the nineteenth to be exact. Rose had gone into false labor twice already so I figured that this morning's episode of cramps and tears were more of the same, so I went back to sleep. Truth be told, I honestly believed she was putting on an act the other two times to see if my daddy would come running, and he did… straight to the hospital like a man whose pants were on fire. I could see the hurt on Rose's face when he'd leave after the doctor announced false labor. She didn't hide it well.

This day was different; my Momma had come to me in a dream and told me that he was coming. She said, "*Desi, come sit down next to me Muffin. I need you to do me a big favor, go easy on your mother; she's in a lot of pain right now, and she is going to need your help.*" I nodded my head in understanding.

"*I raised you to have respect for your elders, even the ones that mistreat you,*" I begrudgingly nodded again. "*Things might get bad for awhile, but God is gonna see you through.*" I didn't nod.

"*I promise you he will Desiree. Have I ever lied to you?*" I shook my head no and she patted my leg as she stood. "*Good. Now that that's settled, go meet your baby brother. He's waiting for you.*"

As I reached for a hug, she stopped me and said, "*Remember that prayer I taught you? You know the one about the man named Jabez?*"

I nodded again. "*Well remember why he was called that. Say that prayer every day along with your regulars,*" she warned before fading away into oblivion.

With that, I awoke once more to the sound of Rose crying a soft mumbled cry. I got out of bed and pressed my way into her bedroom where she lay in a pool of liquid. She was in a paralyzed state and screamed out that her back was being ripped out. Her legs were visibly trembling; her arms gripped around her belly. I ran to her side and yelled for Michael to come help me. While Rose lay on her back, the movement in her midsection was something out of a horror movie. Her skin stretched and poked almost violently. I could see the baby's foot print wildly kicking near her breast.

When Michael finally entered the room, he froze. I screamed at him to help me turn her on her side. "*MICHEAL PAUL PENDER GET YOUR ASS IN GEAR!* Help me turn her on her side!" He snapped out of his momentary trance and rushed over to the other side of the bed. I pushed and he pulled and Rose let out a blood-curdling scream. I immediately noticed the crimson fluid gushing from the area between her legs.

"Go get help! Call somebody!" I screamed in absolute horror. I'd heard that childbirth was gross, but this was downright disgusting.

Michael let go of our mother and passed little Kenneth, who had entered the room unknowingly. It felt like he was gone forever. I held Rose's hand and did my best to comfort her. "It's ok. You're ok. Just breathe." I swallowed hard trying not to cry.

"Momma Elizabeth said you're gonna be fine."

All Rose could get out was a barely audible whimper that turned into a full-on stifled cry. I couldn't wait for Michael to return. I had to do something. So I said a quick prayer and propped a few pillows behind her head and near her back.

I remember Aunt Juanita telling me that having a baby was like taking a hard shit. Her words not mine. So I figured you had to be in the right position to make it come out. I rolled her onto the pillows and told her to open her legs to let him out. I inched her body over as I pulled her backwards. The task proved to be more than she and the baby could handle, but she did as I instructed. As her legs dropped to the side, the head of the baby began to emerge.

"I can see him! *Push like you gotta take a shit!" I yelled.* "Keep pushing! I can see it!" With three hard heaves this ball of gook came gliding out of her worm hole as if that was all he was asking for, to be let out.

I'd forgotten Kenneth was in the room and I tripped over him trying to get to the slimiest mess I'd ever had the misfortune of witnessing. Kenneth started a whiney cry, and I quickly turned and yelled a sharp, "*Shut up*," before continuing with my task. Surprisingly he did as he was told.

An exhausted and sweaty Rose lay still for a little too long for my comfort. I didn't know what to do so I sat down next to her and patted her flushed cheeks, "*Rose. Rose.* Keep pushing something is still attached." She didn't respond. My eyes watered and her face became more of a blur with each pat until I felt a sharp tug on my arm; there was our neighbor and Michael.

I stepped out of the way and pulled both of my brothers close to me. We watched every pain-staking moment of our mother's rescue.

"I called your aunt's house and an ambulance," he informed me. Without another word, he scooped the baby in his arms and wrapped him in the blanket hanging off the end of the bed. The rope-like cord that bound my mother and brother together was still attached and swinging loosely. That's when my father appeared; he was visibly shaken and out of breath. Rose had passed out and looked like death was taking over her body, one inch at a time.

My daddy took the baby and pulled something from his nose, swiped his finger in the baby's mouth and pinched him. The baby started to cry.

Our neighbor was doing his best to perform CPR on my mother until the paramedics arrived. They whisked Rose and the baby away, but not before cutting the umbilical cord and pressing her stomach to force the baby yoke out of her body. I did my best to sooth my crying siblings and assure them that Rose was going to be just fine. I told them, Momma Elizabeth had told me so and she would *never* lie to me and, I would never lie to them.

He was a perfectly healthy chunky bouncing baby boy. It was a miracle that either of them survived. Rose was in no condition to name him so my daddy did the honors. She spent two weeks in the hospital, but Derrick was home in a day or so. My daddy came to stay with us, and I helped with the baby as much as I could.

My daddy said he'd name him Derrick Thomas Pender after Rose's father, my beloved Poppa, and Jacob's father respectively. He always said those were men who commanded respect and their names were just as strong as they were. I overheard my aunt Juanita ask him if he was sure that he should give the baby our family name since he wasn't sure if Derrick was actually his or not.

My daddy dismissed her just that same way he

did when people speculated about Kenneth, "He's mine," he said with authority and flashed that proud father smile he liked to flash when people spoke of his children.

Personally, I liked it when Jacob spoke of past relatives. It made me feel more connected to a family I'd been deprived of knowing due to the circumstances of my birth. At any rate, I always knew he felt terrible about everything that happened to me and to Michael, but I also knew he felt just as powerless when it came to Rose Thorn. He often joked that Rose was the permanent thorn in his side, like a punishment and a gift from God.

I never understood their relationship...*ever*... which is why it wasn't a big surprise that the day Rose came home, she put my father out *again*. She yelled all through the house about not needing his help and never wanting him in her life. *That was clearly a lie.*

Right then and there I decided the military must've made the both of them certifiably crazy.

7

Exactly one week to the day that Derrick was born, my Poppa Derrick Thorn passed away. He slipped away during the night and I felt him leave. My body shuddered under the intense feeling that I was losing yet again. I awoke to a tear stained pillow, a sleeping Derrick Thomas under my arm and the coldest feeling in my heart. And next I heard the sound of Rose crying so very loudly it shook Derrick.

There was no need to get up. I already knew what had happened; I saw it in my dream. I was just happy he'd kissed me goodbye before joining Momma Elizabeth.

I guess this is what Momma meant when she told me things were gonna get worse before they got better. I sighed deeply as I stared at my bedroom ceiling wondering what could possible happen next.

The funeral was eventful to put it mildly. Everyone on Poppa Derrick's side of the family placed a single red rose on his coffin. This gesture did not set well with Pam... it was apparent by the scowl on her face as each person laid their flower gently atop the coffin and made a reference to him being joined in eternity with Momma Elizabeth. There were lots or arguing, fighting, and accusations about murder and who had a right to what.

The biggest mystery for most of us was: *Did Pam Brown-Thorn, my grandmother's best friend, really poison her? And did my Poppa know about it? And was Pam's youngest son really my Poppa's son?* I'd never met him or at least I don't remember ever meeting him, but from what I gathered he was born a thug and was in prison for armed robbery.

It's hard to believe a family that was once so normal, would be caught up in blasphemy this twisted and unbelievable, but yet here we were. Pam decided who got what. Needless to say, she didn't leave my Poppa's real kids with a pot to piss in or a window to throw it out of. However, at the repast, she did give me my grandmother's apron and a set of her hair combs.

For some reason, completely unexplainable to everyone present, Rose became enraged about this gesture. She called Pam a *"worthless bitch"* and then demanded that I give her the items Pam had given me.

Unfortunately for Rose, I was having no parts of her foolishness. Elizabeth Thorn was *my* Momma and these were her things, and Rose would have to pry them from my cold dead hands. I was not going to give them up willingly!

She must have read my mind because she attacked me like I was some stranger on the street who had stolen something from her. I whooped her ass that day!

I hate to admit it, but it felt good! I took out every piece of aggression I'd harbored toward her in a five-minute fight. She did her best to give me a run for my money, but we went from the back of the house to the front yard while my family made very minor attempts to break us up. By the time, we landed on the front lawn, I'd had her neck between my palms and attempted to squeeze the life out of every inch of her body before Jacob pried my hands from around her throat. He pulled me off of her using a bear hug maneuver.

"I HATE YOU! I HATE YOU! I HATE YOU!" I screamed as I punched, wiggled, and kicked. Jacob was strong, and I knew when I'd met my match so I stopped fighting and he set me down.

My tears fell like Niagara Falls and the snot drained from my nose; I hugged him tight and buried my face into his shoulders. "*Why* does she hate me so much? *Why* is she so hateful? I didn't ask to be here..." My voice was now hoarse from yelling.

"She doesn't hate you....she's just got issues," My daddy said, as he tried to comfort me.

I stayed with him that night and cried in his arms until I fell asleep. The next evening I went home to check on my brothers only to find that Rose had locked me out of the house... so I went to the neighbor's house to wait.

This was the same man that merely a week before, had helped save my mother and brother's lives. He was tall and about twenty years older than me. His name was Jerry Minor. It was cool out and

I had nowhere else to go. I didn't want to bother my father or my aunt; I'd caused them enough trouble already. As the night drew to a close, I had to muster up the courage to ask him, "Do you think I could please sleep on your couch tonight? My mother is not well right now and..."

"Yes, that's fine. No need to explain, I've lived next door to your family long enough to understand."

"Please don't touch me."

"You don't have to worry about that either, I promise. You can trust me. You're safe here," he said honestly. "I would never touch you."

My guard was always up because it had to be. In my short time on Earth, I'd already had to fight off three rape attempts, so it was fair to say I didn't trust most men. His eyes were honest and pure, and I looked at him differently that day.

I slept at the house next door for a few hours. As the early morning sky crept through the clouds, I informed Mr. Minor that I was going to go home because I had to go to work. He walked me to the door and as I exited he said, "You be careful young lady."

I nodded and looked over at our house. I saw Rose sitting on the front porch smoking a cigarette. I approached with caution as I studied her face.

When I came across the yard, a bruised and scar-faced Rose awaited me. I looked her in her eyes, and noticed she'd been crying. I didn't stop to make small talk, I just walked passed her and into the front door.

The next thing I heard was crisp *click*. I

stopped dead in my tracks as I felt the barrel of a cold steel piece against my temple. She had put a gun to my head and ordered me back outside and into the car.

"You're getting the fuck outta my house tonight," she said with all of the contempt from the depths of her belly.

"Why are you pointing that at me? All you had to do was say you wanted me out," I said as calmly as I could.

"Shut up! You don't question me."

"Where are you taking me?"

"Since little miss Juanita got so much to say about how I raise mine, she can have your fast ass."

"So you're just gonna push me off on another person. Just kill me now then!" After making that assertion, I sat in an angry silence giving a side eye to her and the gun still pointed at me.

"I'll blow your brains out if you ever think you're going to embarrass me like that again!" she yelled.

"Just kill me then!" I shouted back. My blood boiled with rage. "Just do it!" She was the single person causing all the problems in everyone's life; not just mine. *How dare she threaten me like that! I should be the one holding the gun to her head.*

"Don't think I won't!" She said pulling up on the curb in front of my Aunt Juanita's house. She knew that my daddy wasn't home from work yet. Juanita heard the commotion and came running out of the front door.

"What the *hell* is wrong with your crazy ass?!" She shouted as she approached the car resting but still running in the middle of the sidewalk. When she saw the gun at my head, she stopped cold. "Rose put the gun down."

"Get the fuck out of my car," she ordered. "She's all of yours now!" Rose shouted at Juanita.

I slowly reached for the door handle and eased my way out. Although I was petrified from this whole ordeal, I wasn't afraid to die. I did wonder if she was ballsy enough to pull the trigger when my back was turned.

Without thinking, my aunt grabbed me and shielded my body from Rose's direct line of fire. She never got out of the car. She put the car in reverse without closing the passenger side door and sped away. My aunt stood there holding me as tight as Momma Elizabeth used to; I couldn't even hug her back. One long-running tear streamed down my face and now rested on Juanita's shoulder. That was the last time I ever shared a living space with my mother.

Once we were safely inside the house, my aunt called Jacob at work and told him what had just took place; within the hour he was home. He came barreling through the door and when he found me, he grabbed me and held me once again for the second time in a matter of days.

"What do you see in her? They say she cheats on you like forty going North," I asked seriously.

"Stay out of grown folks' business Desi," she said looking me squarely in the eyes, that look spoke volumes. She was trying to tell me something without telling me. She turned and looked at my daddy and said with a tilted brow, "Nobody wants to think of themselves as someone who's being played."

This time, he made no excuses for Rose Thorn. The realization that she was going to destroy him and our family with all of her shenanigans began to settle into the pit of his stomach and finally resonate with his brain. He apologized for leaving me with her and promised to make sure I would never hurt like that again. I believed him.

8

A couple of months had passed and I was the happiest I'd ever been in my teen years living with my favorite aunt Juanita. She was so caring, loving and understanding. She treated me like a person and more importantly, like I was her daughter. I could talk to her about anything, and I could trust her. That was so very refreshing.

My job at the theater was going great. School was great; my social life was picking up and my brothers were being taken care of. I'd met a really nice man by the name of Clyde Moore when Derrick was born; he was the ambulance driver. He was a few years older than me and really interested in being the man in my life.

As for Rose, well, the week she put me out, she moved Joe McPherson in. Who is Joe, you ask? Yeah, we wanted to know too! It was yet another scandal with Rose Thorn's name attached.

Joe was a country old white man who owned a local auto body shop. He was hated by most of the black community for being a racist and hated by the white community for having many scandalous relationships with black women. The irony was just too much. Apparently it was Rose's turn to take a ride on the Joe train.

I checked on my brothers every day just like my daddy did. I'd take them to school and watch after them until the neighbor girl would show up to babysit them until Rose came home. Michael was on the football team and really into girls. He became more and more handsome with each passing year, and I adored him--so did the girls. All that boy ever did was play football and talk on the phone with the latest flavor of the week.

Kenneth was just as sweet as a kid could be. He was such an innocent little boy who just liked to play and laugh; I pinched his cheeks every time I got the chance.

Then there was Derrick; a sweet little bundle of joy with fat cheeks and bright eyes. But sometimes I swear something was wrong with him. He didn't fuss much, but he'd put on a show every time Joe would enter the room. I truly believe that babies have a sixth sense about people; he *did not like* Joe whatsoever.

I visited Rose's house after work one day and there was a brand new motorcycle sitting in the yard. Joe was on the porch with Kenneth. He was shooting beer bottles off of a partial fence in the yard. Joe had Kenneth lining them up and picking them up as when they fell.

"Don't *ever* have him out there doing that!" I said running over to Kenneth. "What if you make a mistake and shoot him?!" I said disgusted, as I took my little brother into the house and called my daddy. I told him what was going on and expressed my concern about bullets ricocheting.

My daddy rushed over. When he arrived he walked straight up to Joe and looked him square in the eyes and told Joe, "If something happens to Kenneth or any of my sons for that matter, you're gonna be a dead son of a bitch."

"No harm no foul Jacob," Joe said nonchalantly looking away. "Just getting some target practice in."

Without any further hesitation, my father socked Joe in the face. "A dead son of a bitch," he repeated.

I personally believe he was trying to make something happen to Kenneth but, because he was old enough to talk, Joe couldn't do too much to him. From that day, Joe stayed away from Kenneth.

A week or two later, I made my usual stop at the Thorn residence and Joe was there. I heard Derrick crying from the side walk. I ran into the house and into his bedroom, and there was Joe standing over him. I pushed him away and took Derrick in my arms to calm him.

Joe walked out without saying a word; his face had a creepy smirk spread across it as he exited. I went into Michael's room and laid him down next to me. I figured Derrick and I both could use some rest; I wasn't sure how much time had passed, but the next thing I knew, my mother snatched him from me.

She said, "If Joe wants to get him, he can!" Derrick immediately started screaming. Like I said, babies have a sixth sense about people.

There were several odd incidents that caused Aunt Juanita and Jacob to intervene on Derrick's behalf.

Jacob made an agreement with Rose to help her out more and "give her a break" from the kids; he'd take them every other week. At first she was reluctant and then she agreed when my daddy told her this would help them have a better relationship. I was actually proud of him; he was learning how to play her game.

The summer came and I graduated. Jacob didn't like that Clyde was always around when he wasn't. But I enjoyed spending time with him; he was a breath of fresh air, although he was pressuring me to marry him. I wasn't ready for that, I was too young to be anyone's wife, but I also knew it was time for me to go out on my own.

He called Jacob and Juanita and asked if he could meet with them, to my surprise, I walked in the door and there they were sitting in the living room chatting. After a few awkward moments of conversation, my daddy asked to speak with me in the kitchen.

"Listen, I know you're growing up and you're becoming a wonderful young lady, but I gotta be honest. I don't like this guy one bit." He confessed.

"Why?"

"Something about him rubs me the wrong way," he answered, "How do you feel about him?"

"He's alright I guess. If I had to marry somebody, I guess he would be a good choice."

"It's your choice Desi. It's your life."

"Thank you for saying that." I hugged him tight, and we went back into the living room and closed out the evening.

From that point, things just got crazier and

crazier. I was in my bed sleep and Rose came into my room, "Wake up; it's 9 a.m."

"Huh? What are you doing here?" I asked rubbing my eyes.

"You're getting married today."

"What?" I thought she was joking. I wasn't ready for marriage, I was barely nineteen! When I walked into the living room, there was a preacher, Clyde, Jacob, Juanita, and Rose. Before I could blink, I was married to Clyde and within another two weeks he'd be whisked off to Italy with the Army.

Before his pending departure, we went to the local grocery store to purchase some items for the long trip ahead. Rose walked; my aunt told me *not* to say a word to her. So I went to the corner of the store and started playing a video game.

She walked directly over to me and said, "I know you see me *bitch*, don't act like you don't!" She spoke with such a growing anger it made me pause and stare at her. "When you see me you better speak. I'll fuck you up like a bitch on the street 'cause that's what you are to me."

I asked God to give me another five minutes to forget who she was one more time so I could whoop her ass again. I dismissed her threats; I had other things to worry about like Clyde was leaving for the Army and wanted to get things settled before I joined him in Italy. He told me that he wanted me "to come overseas to be with your husband." *Husband*, that had a nice ring to it.

I gathered from Rose's actions that she might have been a little jealous that I became a wife before she did. Although this was my belief, I also believed that she was finally happy for me. What other reason would she have for insisting Clyde and I get married right away? I was shocked that Jacob had even informed her of Clyde's intentions to marry me. At any rate, I was a wife and I had to start getting to know my husband. I stayed in the states until my nineteenth birthday.

9

While I prepared to leave the place I called home, Derrick was going through torturous hell. He was always having an accident at least once a week, and they usually involved Joe. I remember one of the worst was the week before I was leaving for Italy.

The girl next door would babysit until I got there because Rose worked nights. This particular evening, when I walked up the steps of the front porch and came into the house, everything was eerily silent. Rose had given Derrick my old bedroom at the very end of the hall.

As I entered I called out to him, but there was no sound; he usually responded very well to my voice. The room was dark as I entered. I turned the light on and looked over into the bed; there was my baby brother, laying motionless on a cracked and separated bed. His head...it was so big...it looked like an adult's head on a small baby.

I screamed so loud that I woke the neighbors before I took off running.

"Michael Paul! Michael!" I screamed. When Michael came running into the bedroom, I almost slapped him on site. "What happened?" I said shaking him.

"I don't know. I didn't do it," he swore as he leaned over to look at our disfigured little brother. Before he could say anything else, I shoved him aside and took off in a full sprint towards the sitter's house while Michael dialed 9-1-1. As I made it across the three lawns that separated us from her, I burst through the front door of her house. I snatched the girl by her throat and slammed her head against the wall.

"What the hell did you do to my brother!?"

"*I-I...*" She stuttered trying to regain her vocals.

"You better start talking before I send you to meet your maker!" I shouted. "What happened to my brother?"

"I don't know!" She shouted back through hard tears. "I put him down for a nap and he's been sleep the entire time. You can ask Joe, he went in to check on him before he left."

My attention shifted drastically when I heard the piercing sound of the ambulance's sirens approaching. I sprinted back across the same three lawns I'd crossed and into the house. The paramedics loaded him onto a gurney and shoved Michael and I out of the way.

"Go get Kenneth and stay with him 'til Rose gets here!" I ordered. "I'll call Jacob!" I said running to the phone. I jumped in the back of the ambulance and watched in a haze of confusion and terror as I begged God to spare him. My baby brother's spirit was fighting for his life on the short ride to the hospital; I could feel it in my soul.

When we arrived, I was shoved aside and told to wait while they rushed him into the back. Jacob was there soon after, demanding answers from the nurses at the nursing station. No one had answers, but there were plenty of questions.

A couple of police officers pulled my daddy aside and asked him a multitude of questions about the incident. My daddy was so flustered that he couldn't really answer anything other than to say, "Ask Rosie. Find Rosie. I don't know...I just don't know..."

My anger continued to brew from my core and was rapidly approaching my boiling point. I had to get out of there. "Excuse me, officer," I said in the most polite voice I could muster, "I have to get back to my other brothers. Is it ok if I go check on them?"

"Sure, you can pretty lady." Officer Gold responded.

"Thank you. I'll let Rose know to get here as soon as I can find her," I advised my daddy with a kiss on his cheek. He looked as if all the blood had drained from his face.

"I can drop you off...*Ms*?" Officer Gold said looking into my eyes with a smile.

"That would be nice, thanks! And it's *Mrs.* Desiree Moore; Derrick Pender is my baby brother."

"Oh?" Officer Gold said inquisitively.

"Recently married." I answered quickly before he could ask. "*Uh*, I was told by the babysitter that Joe McPherson was the last person to be with the baby."

"*Joe!*" Jacob yelled.

"Sir, keep it down," The other officer said in a hushed voice. "Are you referring to the Joe McPherson that owns the body shop in town?"

"Yes, the one and only. My mother has been dating him and ever since he came around Derrick started having 'accidents'," I informed the pair.

"Now why would anyone want to hurt an innocent child? Especially a well-respected business owner like Joseph McPherson?"

The aggravation on my face must have been overly apparent because Officer Gold immediately redirected his questioning to my father, "We will look into this matter. Where can you be reached if we need more information?"

Jacob gave them contact information. I tapped Officer Gold's hand and politely asked, "Can we go now?"

I left the hospital that night feeling like I did a few years earlier. No one did anything. The police shrugged it off as an accident probably from climbing out of his crib. Rose was pissed because I blamed Joe; my daddy was pissed that Rose would allow Derrick to be subjected to such abuse. He started proceedings to get custody of the boys.

The day I left, my daddy and aunt drove me to the airport.

"I know you don't need my advice or anything but please do everything you can to get my brothers away from that psycho."

"You shouldn't call your mother that, Desiree." Aunt Juanita cautioned.

"I'm not talking about her. I'm talking about

Joe," I said matter-of-factly.

"I will take care of it. Right now you just need to worry about getting on that plane and being a wife...it still doesn't sound right to say that about you," Jacob frowned.

"I love you so much Daddy. Clyde is a good guy and I'll be fine," I said trying to sound convincing.

"But I'll tell you this, if you don't get Derrick away from Joe and Rose, the next time y'all talk to me, Derrick is gonna be dead," I warned.

"Stop talking like that!" Juanita snapped.

"I love you both. I have to go," I said defeated. I hugged them and exited the vehicle.

"She'll be alright; she's young and will learn from this mistake and move on," Aunt Juanita said after turning to Jacob and seeing the tears well up in his eyes.

"I hope she finds the strength within herself to come back home when this goes as bad as I know it will," Jacob said pulling away from the curb.

When I finally arrived in Italy, Clyde greeted me with open arms and promises of a wonderful life as his wife. I couldn't help but cry at the new journey I was about to begin and the old one I'd left behind. Not only was this a new city, but it was an entirely new country, and I didn't even know the language. I was scared and excited all at the same time. I didn't know how to be a wife, but I did know what *not* to do... all thanks to Rose Thorn.

10

I arrived at our base housing and Clyde Moore was all too ready and eager to break my vaginal seal. I'd held my virginity as a gift for the man I was to call my husband, and I was proud of that fact. I'd never really been kissed or fondled for that matter, so my anxiety about this day was causing my stomach to cramp and my body to quiver at random. I was looking forward to it, but I was also dreading it slightly more. I didn't know how to be sexy or what to do other than lay down and spread my legs.

This is normal. This is natural. He's my husband and we have God's blessing. That was what I kept repeating in my head on the plane ride and even as I tried to confidently walk into our home like a woman. *Oh God! What am I doing here! I want to go home.*

You see, being an older man Clyde had much more experience than I did. Although I knew I wasn't necessarily in love with him, to this day I still wish I had waited on all of it -- the marriage, the moving, the sex, the whole damned thing.

I was raised in a place and time where virginity was a sacred thing to only be given to the man you truly felt deserves it; that man was supposed to be your husband, even though that was never the case for Rose. It is one thing that you will never be able to take back after it's given.

We did not consummate our union initially because we agreed that it would take place in our first home together. Not my parent's house or a cheap motel. Since we knew he would start his Italian tour of duty so soon after we wed, he said it would be so romantic if we made love for the first time in a foreign country as beautiful as Italy.

It was a very romantic but painful experience. Becoming a real woman was a task I was not ready for, but knew I could handle.

My first time wasn't physically pleasurable nor was it emotionally satisfying. However, it was an unforgettable memory. Clyde did his best to set the mode with the dim lighting, soft music, and warm room temperature in an attempt to make me feel safe and comfortable. I took a quick shower, put on some lightly scented lotion, slipped on a white negligee after pinning up my hair in a messy bun. I felt pretty, confident and powerful in that moment; don't ask me why, I just did.

We started with some awkward kissing, moved into making out, and held that pace for a while. Instead of relaxing I was so worried about getting it right that I tensed a few times, but he kept going with the foreplay; I became more aroused as the area between my thighs made me feel as though liquid would start to ooze out of my body any moment. I knew it was a natural reaction, but the increased sensation and pulsing was exciting and new.

"Try not to be afraid," he said in a low sultry voice before kissing me again, "Ask for what you need in the moment - don't over think it," he continued.

My heart raced, "Then just be sure to take it slow," I said looking up at him. With those words, he entered me a little bit at a time. It was a little rough at first; although he was extremely careful with me, it hurt. *It hurt like hell.* I wasn't relaxed, and I definitely wasn't into it. I was so nervous that my body locked up and made everything more difficult. He'd officially broken my hymen; I bled a little bit. He slowed down and moved gently to ease the pain of my first time.

Soon after we settled in, he became Dr. Jackal and Mr. Hyde. Clyde Moore became verbally and physically abusive almost immediately. I quickly figured out that he picked me to be his wife on purpose because I was a young immature girl trying to be grown. I knew I had no business with this old ass man in the first place!

It was all too easy for him to snap at the slightest annoyance. When he'd talk down to me; I'd do the same to him. When he hit me, I'd hit him back harder. When he apologized, I'd apologize too. I thought we reacted to each other the way we did because of my immaturity and his insecurities. Never in my wildest dreams did I think he'd ever try to kill me until the day that he actually tried.

It was November thirtieth, and I'd spent the previous night having the angriest and wildest sex of my life with my husband. This type of thing had quickly become our norm. I was late getting up and going to the market to pick up some things I needed for dinner. When Clyde came home, I wasn't there. I walked in shortly after he arrived home. The brown paper grocery bags were heavy in my arms as I struggled to get in the door, "Can you help me?" I said more frustrated than annoyed.

He casually walked over to me and slapped my face; hard. I dropped the bags as I fell to the door. "Don't ever have me waiting," He said forcefully then turned to walk away.

After the initial shock and sting of my face registered, I found my balance and charged after him at full force. I pushed him as hard as I could into the wall near the kitchen. His face hit the door frame with a thud. That's when he turned around and lunged at me with more strength than I had exerted. He tackled me to the ground; I fought him with everything within me. I landed a few punches to his face and upper body before he managed to wrap his hands around my throat.

I scratched and clawed at his face until I drew more and more blood; I finally decided to put an end to all of this. One of us was not going to survive this time. I went for his eyes. I became terrified of blacking out or even worse him killing me; it was either me or him, kill or be killed. He was trained for this sort of thing.

He leaned down in an attempt to apply more pressure to my neck unknowingly getting close enough for me to reach his eyes with my limited force. I put one finger in his eye and his grip loosened ever so slightly. I gasped for a slice of air before forcing my other finger into the other eye. He released me like a hurt animal tending to its own wounds.

What possessed him to do that to me was *and* still is, beyond my own comprehension. What I *did* know was that this relationship was beyond over. My departure was long overdue, but I refused to go back to the states and admit defeat. Something had to give. Clyde Moore was the most awful example of a predator seeking a vulnerable prey.

What rational thirty-two-year-old man would marry a nineteen-year-old girl? I was done with him and the marriage; I just had to figure a way out.

My head and body ached while my mind raced as I lay in bed, contemplating an exit plan that night. At some point, I must have exhausted myself and fallen asleep. I was startled by the loud ringing of the telephone echoing throughout the house. I managed to untangle myself from the bedding and look around; there was no sign of Clyde. The house was completely quiet. The last thing I remembered was gasping for air and crawling toward the bedroom.

As I swung my legs over the side of the oversized bed and jumped down, I stumbled. The phone rang out again and finally stopped. I gingerly made my way into the bathroom when someone began banging on the door.

"Desiree!" *Bam! Bam!* "Are you in there? Are you ok?" The male Italian voice shouted.

"Yes! I'm ok." I yelled out. "I can't come to the door right now Giovanni."

"Open the door. Let me see you."

"Ok. Ok." I said changing direction. I opened the door and immediately began to cry in his arms. Giovanni was an older man, even older than Clyde. He was the first person who had befriended me in Italy; we met at the market and I discovered he was my neighbor. His was a widower and simply enjoyed teaching me about the culture. I enjoyed learning.

When he met Clyde, he said, "Clyde è una minaccia! Non si deve essere con lui una bambina." [Translation: *Clyde is a menace! You should not be with him young girl.*]

I was shocked by such an immediate assertion, but I did value his opinion.

He stepped inside and closed the door. I continued to cry as we sat in the parlor of my small house. "You were right Gio, I should have listened to you. He *is* a *minaccia*!" I cried; Giovanni handed me a handkerchief from his pocket.

"I'm just glad you're alive *bambina*!" He said clearing his throat. "I heard the commotion and called *le forze di polizia!*" I looked at him and saw tears welling up in his eyes, "Ma non prima che i ragazzi e mi sono rotto alcune ossa." [Translation: *But not before the boys and I broke some bones.*]

I smiled at him and hugged him tight, "You broke his bones?" I asked seriously. "Which ones?" I chuckled. "Don't worry about that," he said hugging me tighter. I jumped when the phone rang once more.

"Excuse me, someone has been trying to reach me all day." I answered the phone almost annoyed. "*Ciao*."

"Hello. May I speak with a Mrs. Desiree E. Moore?" The smooth voice on the other end of the line was not one I recognized.

"This is she."

"Mrs. Moore, this is James Taylor, I'm calling from the American Red Cross here in the US."

"Yes, what's this about?" I asked nervously.

"Unfortunately, I am a volunteer and I can't discuss this matter over the phone. However, there was an unfortunate accident involving your brother Derrick. Your presence has been requested immediately and we've arranged transportation for you."

My stomach dropped and I felt sick. "Derrick...what happened? Is he ok? Is he dead?"

"Ma'am I sorry, but I don't have additional information at this time."

"Please just tell me..." I began to cry, "How do I get home?"

His voice was calm and empathetic, "We'll send a car service for you within two hours to take you to the airport. You're flight has been booked and paid for by the Red Cross."

"I can be ready." I said glancing over at Giovanni, who was now standing with a look of sincere concern, apparent by the stress lines above his brow. "Thank you for calling."

"You're welcome. There will be someone to meet you when you're flight lands."

"O-Ok..." My mind went blank, "What did you

say your name was again?"

"James Taylor. I'm a volunteer here. I'm sorry I can't be of more assistance," he said with empathy.

"No...uh...I'll be ready when the car arrives." My body responded to his calming voice. I felt time momentarily freeze as I breathed in deep and exhaled. A few tears escaped my eyes, but before they could hit the floor, Giovanni was taking the phone from my hand and hugging me.

"Something is wrong with my brother," I sobbed with my face buried into his shoulder.

"I can't handle anything else. Oh God! What did he do to my baby brother?" I felt my knees get weak against an instant support.

"What did they say?"

"I have to be ready in two hours to go back home. Something terrible has happened to my brother Derrick. I have to go home."

"Well let's get your bags packed. You don't need to come back here."

"What about Clyde? I can't just leave my husband."

"Yes you can, and you will," He said sternly. "Get a divorce and move on with your life before that man kills you!"

His words were sobering...*before that man kills you.*

11

The eleven hours, thirty five minute flight from Italy to the United States was rattled with waves of nervousness and confusion. I had no information about my brother, and I had no idea what to do about my husband. I applied mounds of makeup to my face and neck and covered the rest of my body with clothing, that way the bruises wouldn't show.

Giovanni promised me that Clyde wouldn't be giving me any more trouble. He even went so far as to promise me that Clyde would be all too eager to sign whatever papers needed to absolve myself of this treacherous marriage. The heat in my face came and went fast and furiously throughout the flight. My tears were uncontrollable, but I managed to keep the sound down to a low murmur so as not to disturb any of the other passengers.

Once I arrived into the US, I was greeted by a handsome young man holding a sign bearing my name, *Desiree Elizabeth Moore*. He was dressed in casual office attire and stood about six feet two inches. His eyes were an exotic mixture of hazel and bluish green. He was fit, but not overly muscular; he was what we called mulatto or of mixed decent. He had a striking aura, but not because of his physical features; it was something else...a feeling or reserved strength that emanated from his mere presence.

"I believe I'm the person you're looking for," I said walking up to the gentleman.

He glanced at the sign then back at me. "Are you Mrs. Moore?"

"Yes. Can you take me to my family, please?"

"Of course," he said starring into my eyes. "Of course, come this way," he said as he reached for my bag and I followed. "My name is James by the way, we spoke on the phone."

"Nice to meet you, James..."

"Taylor. James Jones Taylor."

I smiled at his confidence, "It's good to place a name with a face."

"I'm glad this name and face could bring you a small note of peace," he offered nodding his head at my smile. "You've got dimples too," he continued as if he'd made a previous statement to attach that one to.

"You noticed."

"They're hard to ignore," he said facing forward.

"I'd say the same for your voice," I blurted out, "What I mean is, your voice was calming even though you were calling to give me bad news," I followed trying to clean up my sudden embarrassment. "So did you know you were going to pick me up?"

"No, not at the time...but...you sounded like you could use a friend, so I asked if I could handle the task."

We walked in silence until we reached the car. My heart thumped and eyes were red from crying. Thoughts of Derrick began their sprinted pace through my head again. The momentary reprise provided by Mr. Taylor's presence was just enough to settle me until the silence began again, "Do you have more information about my brother now?" I asked trying to prepare myself to be brave.

"I have instructions to take you to the hospital," he simply stated.

"Where are my parents, Jacob and Rose?"

He didn't answer.

"Did you hear my question?"

"Yes."

"So do you know the answer?"

He didn't answer.

"You're scaring me."

"I'm sorry for that...I'm not trying to. It's just...I'm a volunteer who is not trained in dealing with such circumstances; I'd rather the correct person answer your questions."

"Is my brother alive?" I asked slowly.

"Yes…" he said unsure.

The duration of the drive was met with a painful quiet that solicited unspoken questions and received unspoken answers. I knew Derrick was in pain somehow. I knew my parents had been involved and were probably at fault, and I also knew that the next moment was going to be my worst.

When we arrived he hopped out of the car and said, "Stay here until I get back," before he closed the door and anxiously got out of the car. There was no way I was going to stay there! I had to see. I had to know. Just as I was about to exit the vehicle James ushered me into the waiting room and handed me off to a nurse named Kimberly in the waiting area.

I remember how much I appreciated her sympathetic brown eyes that complimented her round face and tall frame. I don't recall anything she said to me before walking me into the intensive care unit where my brother rested. I remember her lips moving and hearing the sounds of machines beeping as we walked passed room after room.

We stopped at Derrick's room, I looked at her for permission to enter, and I saw tears on her face. I breathed deep and slowly, stepped inside and pulled the curtain away. There was a nurse sitting next to his bed saying a prayer; her name tag said Sherry and she was holding a pair of rosary beads. She looked up at me and came around the bed to embrace me.

Derrick lay still. There was no movement or life anywhere in the room. His head was so big; it looked like someone had replaced his with an adult's. There were tubes and bandages all over him. As I scanned his body, my eyes stopped at the two casts--one on each of his arms-- and I could see his fingers were black and blue.

My cry became a stifled scream that I was certain only God himself could hear. My body shook uncontrollably until everything went black. My body hit the floor with a thud.

"DOCTOR JAMES! DOCTOR JAMES!" Nurse Sherry shouted.

"Check her vitals," Nurse Kimberly directed.

"She's not breathing correctly," Sherry said as she checked for a pulse. "I need oxygen now!"

"DOCTOR JAMES!" Kimberly shouted. "*DESIREE!* Can you hear me?" she said as frantically calm as only a trained professional could. They adjusted my body as they placed an oxygen mask over my nose and mouth.

Dr. Alexcia James, along with at least five more people, came running into the room.

"Her pulse is faint," Sherry informed the doctor as she moved to the side. The panic in her voice became more and more apparent as the seconds ticked by. The team of medical professionals placed my limp body on a rollaway bed and transported me to the emergency room where they began poking and prodding at my body in an effort to stabilize me.

I remember floating away to a place where I watched Derrick laugh and play with Momma Elizabeth and Poppa Derrick. He was so happy and that made me smile, although I could feel myself crying. I wanted to stay there with them, to be happy just like them, so I decided to stay. I lost my pulse and things began to beep uncontrollably as the doctors began to scramble, "I'm starting CPR!" Dr. James commanded.

"You can't stay here Muffin. You have to go back." Poppa said with sadness.

"No. Why?" Although I posed the question, I knew I didn't have a say-so in the matter.

"Because you've got a whole life and purpose that you need to fulfill and you can't do that if

you're here," Momma explained.

I felt heaviness on my chest; my eyes rolled back inside my head. I could hear Nurse Kimberly, "She has extensive bruising all over her body Dr. James, she's almost as bad as her son."

"She's either been in a really bad accident or someone has been using her for batting practice," Nurse Sherry remarked. "Who would do this to a mother and her child?"

My vision was blurred; I could make out an image of Dr. James pushing up and down on my chest. "She's got a pulse. She's waking up. Get her a breathing tube and start an IV. Kimberly, finish her labs and Sherry come with me, we need to find out if she has any internal bleeding from those injuries."

I couldn't speak; I allowed the large droplets of water careening from my eyes down either side of my face, to do the talking for me. Derrick was like my child just as much as Michael and Kenneth were, and I had left them. I had left them just like Rose had left me. I failed them and now Derrick was paying the ultimate price.

A short time later, I could hear Rose's voice shouting like a lunatic, "Where is my baby? I want to see my child now!"

"Ma'am you have to calm down," Nurse Sherry's voice carried with authority.

"Where is my baby?" Rose demanded again.

"Right this way," Nurse Kimberly said taking her arm and guiding her into my room.

"What the hell is *she* doing here?" Rose said sharply.

"She's lost consciousness while visiting her son

in intensive care. From the looks of it, they are both banged up pretty bad."

"*Her son?*" Rose retorted. "This lazy bitch doesn't have any kids. That's my son in there! This is my daughter."

"Oh...I-I..." Nurse Kimberly replied taken aback.

"We thought that—"

"I don't give a fuck what you thought! Take me to *my* son right now!"

"Right this way, Ms.—"

"Thorn." James Taylor said from a distance. "Her name is Ms. Rose Thorn and she is the birth mother of Derrick Pender, that poor defenseless child laying in there fighting for his life."

"Who the fuck are you?" Rose said turning around until her eyes met the man who'd called her out in front of all these people.

"It doesn't matter who I am Ms. Thorn. What matters is that you finally posted bail and now you can see your handy work before you're prosecuted for murder."

"*You did this to your children?*" Nurse Kimberly scolded. "Oh no! Not in my hospital! Call security!"

"I didn't do that to my own flesh and blood!" Rose said with a sneer and a hint of remorse. "You can't stop me from seeing my son."

"Aren't you even going to ask about your daughter?" Dr. Alexcia James asked as she reentered the emergency room.

"No," Rose replied sternly.

"Take her to see her son then," Dr. James

instructed.

TRAUMA CODE BLUE. TRAUMA CODE BLUE. TRAUMA COLD BLUE. The words rang out over the hospital's public announcement system. Dr. James, Nurse Kimberly and Nurse Sherry immediately ran toward the direction of the light blazing above the doorway....

Officially, Derrick Thomas Pender died at 12:07 a.m. on December third, but I knew he was gone hours before.

12

As I lay in the hospital bed, I began to realize I had been beaten nearly to death at about the same time that Derrick was beaten, except I was able to fight back; I survived. Dr. James and another woman quietly entered my hospital room. They stood shoulder to shoulder visually assessing me and whispering. My head pounded like a jackhammer against concrete; my body felt as if it was tied to a boulder that was weighing me down.

"I must look horrible," I said with a sandpaper tongue.

"You're awake," Dr. James replied.

"Mrs. Moore, my name is Sonja Miller; I'm a social worker and I've been working with your family for a few months."

"Desiree, I don't know if you remember me but I was one of the doctors attending to your brother Derrick a few months ago. I also attended to you when you came in yesterday."

"If you're coming to tell me about my brother I already know."

"Actually, Mrs. Moore, may I call you Desiree?"

"Yes, you may."

"I need to ask you a few questions about your family and..." she stopped, as if she were trying to find the least offensive wording, "um...the damage to your personal body."

My mouth was dry and so were my eyes. I literally ran out of water, as was obvious in my voice, "The damage done to my body was compliments of my military husband. The damage done to my brother's body was done by Joe McPherson; I'm sure of it."

"How can you be so sure?" Sonja Miller questioned.

"I think I can answer that," Dr. James interrupted. "When Desiree brought baby Derrick into my ER, she'd told the officers that this Joe McPherson person was the one who assaulted him then." She took a deep breath, "We're a small community here and I can't..." she breathed deeply and exhaled slowly in an attempt to regain control of her emotions, "I can't understand why anyone in their right mind would do this to a child."

"While I respect your opinion, Dr. James, I will need to speak with Desiree alone."

"The only thing you need to know is that Michael and Kenneth need to be with my father, Jacob Pender and not Rose Thorn."

When I said my daddy's name, a chill went up my spine. "Where is my daddy?"

"He is in a holding cell at the police station."

"Why? What did he do?"

"He assaulted Joe McPherson and Rose Thorn."

"*My God*! Is he ok? When can I see him?"

"The police decided not to press charges at this time, but felt like he needed to cool off. Your mother was arrested on attempted murder and child abuse charges."

"What about Joe?"

"What about him?"

"Did he get arrested?"

"*For what?*"

I was becoming more and more agitated by the second. I didn't know what exactly happened, but I did know Joe McPherson was behind it. "Because he is the reason my baby brother is dead!"

"Do you have something against white people, Desiree?"

"What? No... What does that have to do with anything?"

"Your mother already informed me about your hatred for whites and your grudge against Joe McPherson for refusing your sexual advances."

My eyes were a blaze of fire, "Let me explain something to you. I love my siblings. If you think my mother is so goddamned sane, and she told you that we did this or that this was anyone else's fault, why don't you take my brothers from that house until you find out what's really what. Now get the *fuck* out of my room right now," I said through gritted teeth.

"I understand you've been through a great deal of trauma," her mind was already made up. My mother has a gift of making people believe what she wants them to believe.

"You've already decided that what she said was correct. She told you how I was going to react and what I was going to say and you believed her. You made up your mind so this was not an interview."

"She said —"

"Exactly!" I cut her off, "Once again Rose has fooled yet another idiot. I'll tell you what; if you don't get my brother Kenneth out of there, you will find out who is really lying soon enough."

"Yes she has and she's had about enough of you," there was that confidently assertive voice of James Taylor coming from the doorway. For one reason or another Sonja Miller didn't protest. She left without another word.

"What are you doing here?" I asked confused and embarrassed.

"He never left...well...except to go get your father," Dr. James said looking over at him.

"*Jacob.*" My eyes widened as he entered the room behind James. I was so happy to see him that I tried getting out of bed.

"Sit still baby girl."

"I'm sorry. I'm sorry. I'm *so* sorry...Derrick..." he embraced me and my body shuddered at the pain that surfaced both emotionally and physically.

"You look like I feel," He said looking at me. "Who did this to you?"

"You were right about Clyde," I diverted my eyes away from his, "He was all wrong for me. He...He..."

I stopped speaking when I suddenly remembered James was in the room. He was looking straight through me; I felt nakedly vulnerable.

"I'll leave you two alone."

"Thank you so much, James. Thank you for everything," I said sincerely.

"I'm glad I could help. I'll just be outside if you need me, I promised the police I'd keep an eye on him," he winked at Jacob.

"Where are the boys?"

"With Juanita. I wanted to keep them away from this place...from this mess."

"Derrick's body is still here. I think we should go see him."

With a bowed head, he nodded in agreement. I gathered myself and we went downstairs to the hospital morgue to view the body. All we wanted to know was what happened. *What happened to this innocent little baby boy?*

"Daddy, do you know what happened to Derrick? How did he end up like this? I thought you were taking him from Rose?"

"I had them for the weekend. We were having a good time." My daddy slowly began, "I took them to the grocery store with me and I ran into your mother. Derrick saw her and wanted to go with her, but I hesitated because she was with Joe." He started sobbing, "I let him go anyway. I let him go with them."

"The next thing I know I was being told that Derrick was being rushed to the hospital. I rushed over and when I got there, your mother and Joe were standing outside smoking so I confronted her. She said that she went back to the store for some steaks, and Joe came running into the store saying, *Derrick is dead.*"

I almost collapsed again but managed to back

myself up against a wall for support while he continued. "I decked him right then and there. That's when your mother jumped on my back trying to pull me off of him. I threw her into the bushes and commenced to wailing on Joe. I didn't even make it inside to see *my* son," He said crying harder. "*Now look at him.*"

"So you're saying this is my fault?" Rose said standing behind us.

"This *is* your fault and you will burn in hell for it," Jacob said without turning around. "I will hate you forever for this Rose Thorn."

"This was an accident, pure and simple Jacob. He's my son too!"

"All of your children hate you to their core," he responded bluntly turning to look at her face to face. "You will pay for this, you *she-devil*."

I watched Rose's face turn from scorn to distress then actual pain, as Jacob passed her and I followed.

I was released from the hospital that day. James Taylor was there for every moment, and I appreciated having a calming presence around me but not before I had a complete and total melt down as we got to the parking lot. I remember screaming. I remember yelling. I remember punching the car and trying to tip it over. All I could do was fall to the ground.

13

Joe McPherson was finally arrested for the murder of my baby brother Derrick Pender! Led by Jacob Pender, Juanita, Michael, Kenneth and I all filed into the police station as a unit and demanded to see Detective Bryant Rowe. He'd been assigned to the case due to his many interactions with our family over the years. He was one of few who could crack Rose's steel exterior just enough to get through.

Detective Rowe asked the case worker, Sonja Miller, to join us; we each gave a full account of the events leading up to Derrick's untimely death.

With each account of Derrick's short life, a hazy picture began to emerge for Detective Rowe. It was time to confront Ms. Rose Thorn, who refused to believe that Joe had anything to do with Derrick's injuries and death.

I wouldn't call her love struck when it came to Joe McPherson, more like delusional. It was beyond our comprehension how anyone could not put two and two together and get four in this situation.

As Sonja heard story after story after story from the mouths of innocent children and concerned adults, she became more and more uneasy. I suspected she began rethinking her continuous decision to back Rose, who needed someone on her side for the custody war Jacob had waged against her.

Our family watched from an adjacent waiting area as Detective Rowe ushered Rose inside a conference room located at the back of the police station, "Please take a seat, Rosie."

"This isn't a social call Bryant, don't call me Rosie."

"Ok, Rose, I just need to talk to you about some things we've uncovered during our investigation into the death of your one-year-old son, Derrick."

"I know who died and I know how old he was Bryant," she responded coldly.

"Does none of this affect you?"

"He is...was my son, of course this affects me."

"You don't act like a mother interested in the truth."

"And how does a mother who is interested in the truth act? I'm here aren't I?"

"Alright fine, have it your way. You are not under arrest Rose, just answer a few questions and I can let you go."

"Ask away."

"Do you recall an incident where Derrick was admitted to the hospital for a broken arm?"

"Yes."

"Which time?" he said sternly, "No, as a matter of fact, which arm?"

"Derrick was just accident prone. He was clumsy."

"*A one-year-old child?*" he questioned with a raised brow, "Let me switch gears here for a minute. Let's play a game; I'm going to ask you a question and you are going to respond with a name and just a name. *Got it!*"

"Whatever you say, Bryant," Rose said visibly annoyed.

"That's Detective Rowe to you, *ya know* since this *isn't* a social call and all."

Rose rolled her eyes and sat back in the chair. "Ask your damn questions! I hope you do a better job of figuring this out than you did with my mother's death."

"Who was with Derrick the first time his right arm was fractured?"

"Joe was watching him while I went to work."

"Just a name nothing more. Who was with Derrick the night his leg was broken?"

"Joe."

"Who was watching baby Derrick when you found out that he'd hit his head from falling out of his crib?

"Joe," she said softly.

"On the evening of the incident when your daughter took an ambulance ride to the hospital with your son Derrick, who was the last person to handle him prior to Desiree finding him?"

"The babysitter," she said with a smirk of certainty.

"Are you sure about that?" he asked leaning into the table, "Anyone else handle your son that evening before he was discovered?"

"Joe," she said sulking.

"Are you starting to see a common denominator here Rose?"

"Why do y'all keep trying to drag Joe into this? He loves me and my children!"

"Did you know," Bryant thumbed through some papers in a folder on the table, "that the night your son was taken to the hospital with a concussion, he told your son Kenneth, *'I'll do the same thing to you if you don't watch it, boy.'*"

"Why are you lying? Kenneth would have told me that!"

"You are a horrible mother, Rose Thorn. Your children have been abused and neglected right under your nose, and you don't even care to see it. They are afraid of you and your boyfriend. And because of this, I will personally see to it that Jacob gets custody of those boys."

"Fuck you, Bryant!" she said almost laughing.

He opened the door to the room, "Get Sonja in here right now!"

"What is she gonna do?" Rose stood to address her as Sonja entered the room. "Thank God you're here. Can you tell this lovely man that I've done nothing but protect my children?"

"No. I can't do that Rose."

"Sonja," Rose said twisting her lips, "I'm taking my children and I'm walking out of here!"

"If you don't want to be arrested for child abuse and neglect you will sit down and listen," Sonja Miller said looking directly into the eyes of the woman who she once thought was a victim of unfortunate circumstances.

"As of right now, the minor children in your

care, Michael Paul Pender, and Kenneth Jacob
Pender will remain in the custody of Jacob and
Juanita Pender. You are not allowed to make
contact with them or a Mrs. Desiree Elizabeth
Moore. If you do, you will be arrested and thrown
under the jail."

Rose's eyes grew wide, "I—"

"Shout up and sit down! I'm actually doing you
a favor. I could arrest you right now," Detective
Rowe commanded. "Oh and your boyfriend has
already been picked up. He's admitted to beating
your son to death. *To death!*" He repeated.

Rose sat down and began to cry. The pair left
her in the room, and we left. Now it was time to
deal with the aftermath of Rose's bad decisions.

****

My family was finally united again, and I had
the unexpected support of the Red Cross volunteer,
James Taylor. In a strange way he felt like my
protector. I surmised that he felt sorry for me and
my family and felt obligated to see this through to
the end. In my mind, I also decided he was using us
as his case study for law school. At any rate, it was
comforting to have an unbiased person around to
ease the stress of the situation.

James visited my Aunt Juanita's house and
asked me to take a walk with him.

"Thank you for being my peace during all of
this James."

"It's been my pleasure, Desiree. I'm glad I
could be here for you."

"I believe you may know more than you'd like to let on Mr. Taylor."

"You think so?"

"I wouldn't have said it if I didn't."

"What I know is that you and your family have been through the ringer. I've done my homework, but I don't know everything, just what I've read in the files."

"So we're your charity case?"

"No. Not at all. To be honest, when I heard your voice over the phone, I heard pain even before I spoke about the purpose of my call."

"I see," I said looking away, "My father is devastated..."

"And what about you?" he asked genuinely concerned.

"I'm living. I'm breathing...and out of my mind with grief. I'm trying to be strong for everyone.

"Who's being strong for you?"

The questioned jarred me, "I...I...I was glad to be married to get away from it all. My being married was my escape."

"Your husband is your strength?"

"No...*oh* no! My husband is my pain. Like I said, being married was my escape from--"

"*Your escape,*" he repeated. "Is that how you got all of those love marks?"

My silence was the definitive answer he needed. "I guess I didn't do a great job of covering that up huh?"

"No, you didn't, but you shouldn't have to Desiree."

"Thanks for saying that."

"It's the truth," he quickly responded, "I could help you escape from your escape."

"How?"

"Erase him," he said seriously taking note of my reaction, "I don't mean off the face of the earth." He chuckled, "You can get an annulment instead of a divorce. That way it's like it never existed and Catholics will still accept you," he said laughing harder.

"What is that? How can I do that?"

"An annulment is a legal procedure to denounce that your marriage never took place. The annulment process declares a marriage null and void."

"You can't get all technical on me. I'm a simple girl," I giggled. "I wouldn't even know how to do that or where I would even go to get that done."

"You are far from simple and definitely *not* a girl," he smiled. "Don't worry about it. I know a few people, and I'll make sure you get what you need. I'll just need some information from you."

At that moment, I knew with given certainty that James Taylor was going to be my night-in-shining-armor. But first, we had to close out the matter of my brother's funeral.

Yet again our family was the subject of another scandal. As the trial approached, death threats were sent to my mother's house and things became increasingly more violent where she was concerned.

I remember this one evening, I truly felt bad for her being over there all alone; no one would talk to her at all, not even her own family, friends or neighbors, so I went to pay her a visit.

When I arrived, she was laying in bed, wearing a housecoat, staring at the wall. The house was a mess and had a foul odor prancing through it.

"Rose. I think you need to eat something," I said feeling slightly sad for her. She was miserable and it showed. That's the first time I had ever seen her like that in my life.

"I'm going to go fix you something and straighten up a little bit. I'll be right back okay."

She didn't respond. I walked into the kitchen after that to get some order about that place.

As I stood in front of the window at the kitchen sink, the window shattered! Three loud bangs rang out. I screamed and dropped to the floor; someone had shot in the window at me!

Before the silence of the scene settled, I heard someone yell, *"You deserve to die Rose Thorn! Just like that innocent baby!"* as they speed away.

My heart was pounding in my throat. I did all I could to catch the breath that was escaping my lungs. I felt my body for any wounds, but there weren't any, *thank God!*

It suddenly became very clear why Rose was held up in her bedroom in the dark. I cut my knee as I crawled around on the floor until I reached the wall where the light switch and phone rested. I stretched my hand up forcing the handset to fall from the receiver and quickly flipped the light switch in the off position.

I called the police and then my daddy; both came rushing over at about the same time. I hadn't bothered to move or check on Rose; they found me shaking in a corner of the kitchen floor with shattered window pane glass all around me.

14

The trial came quickly. It seemed every adult in the community came to the courthouse to witness the trial of the century. We weren't nervous about the outcome of the trial because Joseph McPherson had confessed to assaulting and murdering Derrick; the truth was on our side. We were however, interested in the *whys* of it all. *Why did he do it? Why Derrick?*

The prosecution and defense took their respective seats, and the trial began. The district attorney began the opening arguments:

"Members of the jury, Joseph McPherson is a killer. And the evidence in this case, will show you that this man engaged in a process of systematic abuse, deception, and concealment.

On November 30th, in the stillness of the early evening hours, in the bedroom of a house in a tight-knit community, a jealous-filled Joseph McPherson did the unthinkable.

You're going to hear testimony that on that day, at approximately 5:15 pm in the afternoon, this defendant came into the bedroom of Derrick Thomas Pender, who is our victim for the second time that day -- once when his mother brought him home from the grocery store, and again after Joseph sent her back to that same grocery store for a steak.

Our victim cannot testify today because he was viciously abused and murdered by the defendant, Joseph McPherson, who will testify about what happened that day.

The defendant didn't steal money from this family, he stole a life from a community. He stole a future from a defenseless child. The man who committed this act is sitting in this courtroom behind me; he's the one who committed this murder. After he did so, he fled the scene; he avoided arrest for a number of days by trying to present this as an accidental death at the hands of a neglectful mother.

Our victim might have run from danger, but he could not; his legs were broken. This is the second time they had been broken during his 14 months of life. In addition his arms had been fractured. This baby was the definition of battered child syndrome. Derrick Thomas Pender died, ladies and gentlemen, with his eyes wide open.

And in the last moments of his tiny little life, Derrick saw his killer but he could not speak; his voice had been taken away.**The last person Derrick Thomas Pender saw through his open eyes was the man who took his young life... the man who now sits in this courtroom, the defendant, Joseph McPherson.

Ladies and gentlemen, we will prove to you that Derrick Thomas Pender died at the hands of the defendant, Joseph McPherson."

The prosecutor boiled the case down to three words: *abuse, deception, and concealment.* These three words kept being repeated by the prosecution during the trial.

My daddy and I were called to testify. We shared our various stories just as we'd done at the police station with Detective Bryant Rowe. My daddy requested that they not ask Michael or Kenneth to take the stand. He felt they'd already been through enough and had seen way too much for children their ages. *I wished he'd been around more when I was their age.*

When Joe was called to the stand, he wasted no time falling apart after being sworn in.

"How did you feel about the victim, Derrick Thomas Pender?"

"I was jealous of him."

"You were jealous of him. Why were you be jealous of an infant Mr. McPherson?"

"Because the woman I love, his mother, Rose Thorn seemed to spend more time with Derrick than with me."

"Are you aware that Derrick was an infant...not yet a toddler and needed his mother to nurture him?

"Yes, but so did I. I wanted her attention. I wanted her to love me like she loved him. She only loved him so much because he was Jacob's actual child. Every time I looked at that kid, all I ever saw was the man Rose really wanted to be with, Jacob Pender."

"Aren't you the father of a son about ten years old?"

"Yes."

"And do you spend time with that son?"

"Yes."

"Yet you physically abused another man's child because you were jealous."

"Yes."

"You, being a parent of a son no less, didn't stop to think that what you were doing to Derrick Pender, another man's child, might kill him?"

"Not at first. I just wanted to hurt him but he was so fragile and he kept breaking so easily."

"In your own words, Derrick was *'fragile and he kept breaking so easily'*, could that be because he was fragile? His little bones did not even have a chance to grow and strengthen before you broke them: abuse, deception, and concealment."

"Every time he got hurt, she would coddle him more. That infuriated me. I love her and she was always focused on him."

"Don't you mean you were obsessed with Rose Thorn?"

"No! I love her."

"Would you agree, Mr. McPherson that love isn't supposed to hurt?"

"Yes."

"Well, according to the medical examiner and all of the thousand pages of Derrick Thomas Pender's medical file, Derrick was delayed in walking at one-years-old because his leg had been broken *twice*! The last thing he felt, Mr. McPherson, was all 197 pounds of you jumping up and down on his little fragile body."

The prosecutor climbed on the courtroom table

and demonstrated how Joe pounced up and down on Derrick's head between twelve to fourteen times. "Then you gave him a bottle and took him to his mother and pretended that you didn't know what had happened! *Abuse and deception!*"

"Yes, I did."

"You then asked his mother to leave and return to the store once more so you could finish the job! *Concealment!*"

"Yes, I did," Joe said evenly.

"Are you aware that *had* Derrick Thomas Pender lived he would have been no good? He would not have been able to lead a normal life because of the brain damage you so graciously inflicted upon him."

"No, I was not aware of that."

"You systematically abused and murdered a little boy because you were jealous of his relationship with his own mother. You jumped up and down on his head fourteen times in a rage, and you can sit on this stand today and casually discuss your actions as if you were recalling your favorite football game."

"Yes, I can because I'm truly sorry that the boy died."

"*That the boy died*...you can't even say his name."

"Derrick Pender."

Quiet tears radiated throughout that courtroom so loudly, you couldn't help but hear the hurt. The jury was excused to deliberate. They came back with a verdict within four hours: *Guilty of murder in the first degree.* For his crimes, Joseph McPherson was only sentenced to fifteen years in prison.

Shortly after the trial concluded, my brother Michael opted for early graduation. My father signed for him to go into the military. He hasn't come back to visit Rose since then. I don't blame him for keeping his distance from her or that small town; our family was the talk of the town for many years.

15

When the trial came to a close, it set in motion a chain of events that changed the lives of everyone involved for the better… everyone except Rose Thorn.

We suffered a great loss with the death of my sweet little brother Derrick. Afterwards things were not functional for a while. I was wrestling with the fact that I could never pinpoint how I had contributed to what was going on; things were unbearable at times.

The death threats slowed, but didn't stop. Rose continued to sit in the dark alone and would only come up for air when Jacob and I brought Kenneth for a visit. Her face would light up for the short time he was there.

I wanted *that* relationship with my mother; hell I wanted *a* relationship with my mother, but we were always like oil and water. She was always giving me away; everyone else raised me. And to make matters worse, she was always defiant with me. She was the adult, but she had no idea how to date or how to have a healthy relationship with anybody.

As time went on, James reminded me that it was time to focus on getting my marriage dissolved. He handled almost every aspect of the paperwork. I told him about Giovanni and the guys in the neighborhood making sure Clyde Moore wouldn't protest anything I requested.

My annulment request stated that I'd gotten married under duress from my abusive mother; I know it wasn't entirely true, but I was willing to live with that little white lie in order to erase this mistake from my life. Being married to Clyde was not only a physical pain, but it became an overbearing emotion that threatened to psychologically damage me.

James encouraged me to enroll in college and go after my dreams, just as my brother Michael had done. It was refreshing having a romantic interest in my corner cheering me on and encouraging me to be the best me, without the pressure of perfection. He waited patiently until my annulment request was processed and approved before finally asking me out on an official date; I gladly accepted his offer.

As expected, he was the perfect gentlemen and this time, Jacob and Juanita approved. Somehow Rose found out about my good fortune and decided she'd ask James over for tea. I forbid him to go or even entertain the idea, and he respected my request and I respected him that much more.

Shortly after that, Rose decided to go back to work. Her car had sat unused for so long that it wouldn't start. Fortunately for her, Pam Brown-Thorn's son, Errick Brown, had been released from prison and was passing through the neighborhood on the way to his mother's house. He couldn't get Rose's car started, but offered to take her to work and pick her up if she'd like. That was the beginning of the end.

The scandal with my brother was still ever-present and now new rumors were surfacing involving those two. It was never confirmed nor denied whether Errick Brown was the bastard child of my Poppa Derrick Thorn; if that were true then that meant Rose Thorn was carrying on an illicit affair with her half-brother!

The thought alone made me cringe. How could she be so desperate for affection that she would actually date her own brother, my uncle? I wasn't going to allow our family to be disgraced anymore due to the shenanigans of the infamous Rose Thorn.

I went straight to her house and asked her face-to-face, "Rose Thorn, I need you to be honest with me about this, I heard a rumor that you and Uncle Errick are seeing each other. Is that true?"

"Mind your own damn business *little* girl."

There was that phrase again, I gritted my teeth and cautioned, "I hope you are not going to embarrass this family any further," I said firmly.

"To answer your question, No, but if they keep talking ,we'll make it true."

"Why would you want to make that true?" I responded in pure and utter disgust, "First of all, he's dating Aunt Angel's friend; he works on your car. And even if you aren't blood siblings, you *are* stepbrother and sister. So no matter what, he *is* your brother!"

"People will always have something to say

about something. Just let them keep talking."

"Are you saying you're actually willing to date your brother just because they're talking about it?"

"If I did decide to do that, it would be my business. What does it matter to anyone else? He's a nice man and he wasn't raised around us."

I couldn't believe what I was hearing! Although I shouldn't be shocked considering when my grandmother passed away (when I was seven), my grandfather married her best friend, Pam Brown, who is *his* mother. This is the same woman who is suspected of poisoning my Momma Elizabeth so she could marry my grandfather!

I left that day and didn't look back; I prayed one day she'd understand her immoral decisions affect everyone.

Rose Thorn always did what Rose Thorn wanted to do no matter what anyone else had to say about it. So my mom went to the local church and asked the family pastor to marry her to Errick. The pastor was *so appalled* by the request that he called a family meeting.

"I've gathered you all here today to personally inform you I will *not* be a part of such foolishness," he announced with conviction, "I baptized and raised you *and* you. You were raised as sister and brother. I will not do this!"

This divided the family for many reasons. I heard so many people say things like: *I hope your mother sees how wrong this is.* Or, *I hope that your mother doesn't get involved with him.* Or, *I heard that he told someone that he's had a grudge against the family and wanted to get back at us. He believes*

that we put his mother through it.
I prayed and cried and cried and prayed for my mother and my family that night.

16

Four years had swiftly passed by. I was blissfully happy, finally leading a normal life. I was living on campus; my relationship with James was nothing short of wonderful.

Michael was excelling in the military and we exchanged letters and care packages religiously. Kenneth was doing well in school and at home and becoming a social butterfly.

Jacob met a nice woman and had been dating her for the past two years, Aunt Juanita opened a small restaurant, and everyone left Rose Thorn to her own devices. We didn't contact her or bother to find out what was going on in her life; our little slice of heaven had a 'Do Not Disturb' sign again above it. Until I flipped that sign over.

I was in class this particular morning when my best friend and roommate, Tina Harper received an urgent message; her mother had passed away. As I listened to her go over the long list of things she could have or should have done and said to her own mother, I couldn't help but think about mine. I didn't want regrets or shoulda', woulda', coulda' moments like the one Tina was having.

I wanted a clear conscience so I confided in my real best friend, James, "I've been thinking… maybe it's time I go visit Rose."

"Why?"

"Because she's my mother."

"Yes and she is also the *only* person who causes you so much anguish at the mere mention of her name."

"Well, maybe in the past, but I'm older and wiser now," I explained.

"Are you sure you want to do this, it may not turn out like you want it to."

"Yes, I'm sure. At the very least I can tell her that I still love her."

"I'll support you no matter what you decide," he said with a deep sigh. "Just know, if she makes you upset, it will make me upset and we will have to correct that situation," he added hugging me tight.

"You always give the best hugs James Jones Taylor."

"You're not allowed to use my government name in intimate settings like this," he chuckled.

"I'm sorry. You always give the best hugs J.J," I giggled, "What kind of name is J.J. for a lawyer?"

The next day I went to visit my mother. I walked up to the screen door on the porch and peeked into the open door. I saw my mother sitting the kitchen while to my surprise, Errick was sitting in a recliner in a bathrobe in the living room. After all that had transpired, I wasn't fond of him.

"Hello," I said ringing the doorbell.

"Come in," Errick said as he sat up. "Haven't seen you in a long time."

"Yeah, it's been a while," I said flatly looking in the direction of the kitchen, "Is Rose in there?"

"I just want to let you know that there will be no loud talking and screaming up in here. It is what it is."

"Um...okay." I said as I continued to walk past him confused. *I didn't come here to argue with her.*

My mother was crying. Rose Thorn was actually shedding real tears at her kitchen table. When she noticed me standing there, she screamed, "Get away from me! Don't come near me!" she said hysterically, "Don't touch me!"

"What's wrong with you?" I asked coming closer.

"Errick told me this morning that he has SYPHILIS!" she said through a series of sobs and hiccups. When she said *SYPHILIS* the words resounded throughout the room, but it didn't totally register with me. See, during this time syphilis was still fairly recent to the black community. She continued, "He says he has SYPHILIS!"

"*What?*" I yelled. "You have what? I thought only people like prostitutes get that disease!"

"Well I'm not a prostitute and neither is he!" She said finally looking at me.

"Oh my God! What are you going to do?" I said looking around, "And why is he still sitting there like he owns the place? Kick him out!"

"When the preacher refused to marry us, we snuck down to Florida and got married," She confessed. "They don't require a blood test."

"YOU MARRIED YOUR BROTHER?" I screamed so loud my ears started ringing; I went nuts! It ran into the living room and punched him on the top of his head.

"What the fuck is wrong with you two?" I said punching him again on the side of his face. I fought him so hard we started in the living room and ended up in one of the bedrooms tussling. Somehow I was on the bed, and I wasn't letting him loose no kind of way. Then, I heard Momma Elizabeth say, *"Let him go before he bleeds on you."* So I released him.

"How could you do my mother like that? How could you?" I shouted through tears that I hadn't realized were coming down my face. He just stood on the side of the bed and looked at me with a blank expression.

"I will never forgive you! You gave my mother a death sentence!" I said returning to the kitchen where Rose was still sitting with her head down.

"You're so goddamned hard headed! I warned you and you just *had* to do it! You're a fool, Rose Thorn!"

"Don't talk to me like that!" she said looking up at me again.

"Shut up! For once your sorry ass is gonna listen," I said sternly. "He came straight out of prison and you knew about all of this drama with his mother! She married Poppa Derrick, get over it because Poppa had to marry her back! Poppa Derrick allowed y'all to be put out and Poppa Derrick left y'all with nothing. Be mad at him! You married that woman's son...your very own brother for God sakes, just so you could get back at her?"

Rose just stared at me. She knew I was telling the truth, "All of this bickering and fighting, all so

Errick could get even and you fall for it!

Think about this; your first marriage is to your brother, 'til death do you part. Congratulations! At least he honored one of your vows."

I left her house and went straight over to Aunt Juanita's to tell them. No one said a word. What else was there to say? Nothing.

Within a matter of months, Rose had gone from a size twelve to a size four; she had gotten so small. Her doctor told me that she could fight this disease, but she is going to die from the shame, the guilt and the fact that I wouldn't forgive her. *Why should I? I didn't owe her a damned thing.* Especially after she said she was going to stay married to him!

Yet another stupid mistake for the Rose Thorn catalogue. Who in their right mind would stay with a man who intentionally gives you a disease because he didn't like the way you treated his mother? He was going to die, and he wanted to take someone with him.

We had a family meeting and decided to leave it alone; these were her choices and there was nothing any of us could do about it.

Without my family's knowledge, I went to speak with Nurse Sherry and Nurse Kimberly. They helped me once, maybe they could help me again. They both pointed me in the direction of Dr. Alexcia James, who connected Rose to some of the best doctors in the area. I didn't want to see my mother die, if I could do something to prevent it.

They accepted Rose into a clinical drug trial. She started looking like herself and wasn't taking any additional meds that we knew of.

While my mother was getting the treatment she needed, Errick was busy finding a new victim. I found out he'd started dating a woman from Florida; they met while she was in town visiting someone. I couldn't allow him to ruin another innocent woman's life so I called her up and told her all about my Uncle/Stepdad Errick.

"Hi, you don't know me but I understand you're dating a man by the name of Errick Brown."

"Yes," she paused, "Who is this?"

"Oh, I'm sorry, I didn't properly introduce myself. My name is Desiree Elizabeth Pender, I'm the niece, oops I mean stepdaughter of Errick Brown. You see, he is married to my mother who also happens to be his sister."

"*What?*" She shrieked.

"You sound surprised. Well if that doesn't kill you, this will. Errick, my uncle, and stepdad respectively has syphilis. Yep! He has syphilis and he gave it to my mother because he is an evil son-of-a-bitch who now wants to pass it on to you."

"I can't believe what you're telling me!"

"I hope you didn't sleep with him yet. And if you did, you should probably go get checked out immediately." I announced before hanging up the phone.

He found out about my phone call and oddly enough, got angry with me, even though he was still married to my mother. It didn't matter, though; she still stayed married to him because she felt like she couldn't be with anyone else in her condition. He obviously didn't feel the same.

Rose was injured at work, and he walked out

on her. Errick Brown woke up one morning and told her he was leaving because he *"was tired of being in a relationship"*. He took nothing but a few of his things and moved north; he basically abandoned her.

"He is showing you how much he cares for you, Rose! Why can't you see that?" I pleaded with her. Until one day she went back to church and the preacher reminded her of 2 Samuel 23:6-7; *But worthless men are all like thorns that are thrown away, for they cannot be taken with the hand; but the man who touches them, arms himself with iron and the shaft of a spear, and they are utterly consumed with fire.*

He continued, "You can be the iron, Rose." The preacher prayed over her and words couldn't express how I felt when she finally listened.

She went to find him, to serve him divorce papers, and find him she did! Rose found out he was now living as a gay man. I mean, he'd always dressed a little weird and he was a lot of things, but I never thought he was gay.

He signed for the divorce and shortly thereafter passed away, but not before he asked – on his deathbed -- Rose Thorn-Brown for forgiveness. She told him that she forgave him. She accepted her life or her fate, depending on how you look at it. It could happen to anyone.

Errick Brown's funeral was a real mess! It was like a pot of coffee at an AA meeting, cold and bitter. I refused to go. I didn't want to be in the same room with all of those people, who are supposed to be my family. For those who weren't around all of these years, the obituary read like a cryptic puzzle. I had to come to the conclusion that life goes on.

There was nothing I could say or do about any of it and worst of all, the family was still divided. It takes two, but they were still mad at my mother.

17

It was a cold winter night during Christmas vacation, James surprised me with a weekend getaway. It was my very first real vacation, and my very first real romantic getaway! He asked me to pack some warm things and be sure to bring my birth certificate. I couldn't understand why, but I did as he asked. Our drive there was filled with long conversations about our futures, but I shied away from anything dealing with my past.

When we crossed the border into Canada, I couldn't believe my eyes. There was something so serene about it. The snow had stopped falling, but the white powdery stuff resting on the landscape was enough to keep me entertained. I just rode in silence for the duration of the drive and admired the natural beauty of Mother Nature.

We pulled into the long driveway at the Loralea Country Inn Resort in Haliburton, Ontario, Canada, where James parked then jumped out of the car while I waited comfortably inside.

My nerves began to get the best of me, because I wasn't sure what to expect. James and I had not made love at all; we only indulged in deep passionate kisses with some minor touching here and there. I was secretly hoping he didn't try anything sexual during our stay, because I knew I wasn't ready for that kind of thing. I knew that I loved him and I knew my body responded to his, but I also knew that my last sexual experience wasn't very pleasant. The silver lining in my mind was at least I could always say it was with my husband. That fact alone would always make me different from my mother.

Once my annulment was final, I was able to pretend that life with Clyde Moore never happened and in my head I took back my virginity; I could start all over again nice, fresh and pure...*in my head. What am I worried about? James wasn't that type of guy; he never pressured me, ever.*

I shook off that thought as his tall frame emerged from the doorway of the registration building. I smiled as I leaned over and opened the driver's side door, "Welcome back!" I said trying not to sound too excited.

"Thanks! Are you ready to have some fun?" He asked getting into the car.

"Of course I am!"

"Let's go get settled in then," he said as he squeezed my hand and then shifted the car into reverse. "I can't wait to get you on a toboggan!"

We parked a short distance away in front of a small cottage house which was situated on the waterfront. We got out, and James escorted me into the country waterfront cottage so I could look around while he retrieved our bags for the car. I breathed a huge sigh of relief when I noticed there were two bedrooms and a sofa bed. I laughed at myself for even being the slightest bit concerned, but I couldn't help it.

When I told Tina what James had told me about packing and the two of us getting away for the weekend she said, "Now you know that means… he is trying to get you to give it up, and if you don't you may lose that man."

I shrugged it off at the time, but once we arrived, I thought for a minute she may've been right. Now that my heart wasn't beating in my throat anymore, I took myself on a tour of the quaint little place. It was cozy, peaceful and warm; there was a small bathroom, full kitchen, living room with a TV and VCR, and the most adorable wood burning fireplace I'd ever seen. Everything had a homey feel to it, right down to the wood planked walls.

I took off my coat and hung it near the door when James reentered, stomping his feet on the welcome mat to dust off the snow that had attached to his shoes.

"Let me help you with that."

"Nope. I've got it."

"You just have a seat while I put this stuff away."

"Are you hungry?"

"A little."

"Good, because I'm going to make you the best spaghetti dinner you've ever had."

"He cooks too! How did I ever get so lucky?" I laughed.

"Fate," he responded quickly.

I did as he requested and went to sit on the love

seat. I watched him masterfully put our things in their respective bedrooms. Then he took a separate bag into the kitchen that had a few groceries hiding in it. He turned on the small radio that was resting on the counter top and found a station with soft music.

Next he proceeded to boil some water and add the noodles. While those were cooking, he unpackaged some ground beef and started to brown it in another pan. However, the part that impressed me most was when he took out some ripe tomatoes and began chopping and dicing. He added them to a boil, sprinkled some seasoning over them, then pulled some fresh garlic from his bag, diced a few cloves before dividing and adding them to the pot of meat and boiling noodles; that was different.

"My my, aren't you just a little chef over there."

He smirked in my direction, "I can do a lot of things for the right person."

A blushed smile spread across my face, and I decided not to respond. He finished cooking then placed the naked noodles on two plates, with a layer of meat and a layer of sauce. He added two drinking glasses to the table and poured ginger ale in both with a few cubes of ice.

"Come and sit here my dear," James motioned as he pulled the chair from underneath the table.

"Thank you."

"So, tell me about your day."

"I was with you all day, silly. You know all about it."

"Do I? Do I really?"

"Unless you weren't paying attention you do."

"Well, what if I told you it was about to get better."

"How could this get any better James Taylor… oops I mean J.J.?"

He paused with a serious look on his face, "First let's say grace."

"*Okay,*" I said suspiciously before I bowed my head and closed my eyes.

"Lord, we come to you right now, thanking you for this food before us, the clothes on our backs, the shoes on our feet and the ability to use them for your glory. I've always been taught that when a man finds a wife, he finds a good thing. I ask that if Desiree Elizabeth Pender says *yes* to being my good thing, that you bless our union for better or for worse."

I heard his words...every single one of them but I was frozen in my chair. *Was this really happening? Did he say what I just heard him say?* I kept my head bowed until I felt his eyes staring at the top of my head. I slowly opened my eyes to James on the side of me, on one knee holding a gold wedding band with an intermediate sized diamond in its center.

"Ms. Desiree Elizabeth Pender, with your father's blessing, I'm asking you to marry me and become Mrs. Desiree Elizabeth Taylor. Will you marry me?"

I couldn't speak. I just sat there in shock until he pulled the ring from the box and placed it on the fourth finger of my left hand.

"Let's eat and toast!" he said getting up from the floor, "I want you to have the wedding you want."

"You make me so happy James. I can't believe my life right now."

"I can say the same for you. I know it's not easy giving your heart...you've been through so much–"

"Let's not talk about the past," I said cutting him off.

"I just want you to know that I understand that you didn't want to let someone close enough to hurt you again. I promise to be the last man you'll ever need, if you just give me a chance."

"I–I...yes! Yes! I will marry you, James Jones Taylor!" I shouted and wrapped my arms around his neck so tight I believe I almost choked him. He kissed me so passionately I thought I was going to give in and lose my born-again virginity before we even make it down the aisle.

There is nothing like love – Nothing like *real* love. I must have stared into his eyes all night because I felt secure in us. I was promised a life of joy, security, and adoration for one small price; I knew I had to be the perfect wife for him.

After gazing at each other over a fantastic spaghetti and ginger ale dinner, we spent the rest of the evening on the love seat chatting about our future when I learned something startling about J.J.

"I have a confession to make," I said honestly.

"Go ahead, confess."

"Tina had me a little freaked out about going away with you...she said that you probably wanted to have sex and if I didn't you'd probably want to break up with me."

"Tina Harper is an idiot."

"She was just looking out for me."

"If you say so," he said slightly annoyed, "Since we are confessing things, I have one."

"Confess your sins," I said jokingly.

"It isn't quite a sin," he said looking at me, "I was never going to have sex with you until you became my wife."

He hesitated, "I've never had sex with anyone ever. I always wanted my first time to be with my wife."

"Well, I can assure you, I'm not experienced either...even though I was married for such a short time." I paused for his reaction. He waited patiently for me to continue.

" I can promise you this much, it's going to hurt me more than it will ever hurt you," I said sheepishly.

"I'm sure we'll figure it out."

18

One year later James and I stood in front of our family and friends on our wedding day and pledged our love and allegiance to each other. When we took those vows we meant them. After witnessing my parents go through all of their trials, I figured I had a scathing example of what *not* to do; I would use them as my road map.

As I held my husband's hands, I could feel him trembling. His six foot, two-inch tall mulatto manliness stood there actually trembling. It made me nervous, and he must have sensed it because he started to go off script.

"It's amazing how I'm standing here, holding my wife's hands, looking like a rock to all of you, but knowing that only she can feel how much I'm shaking. Not because I'm scared of this journey, but because I *never* want to fail her."

I remember that moment; I hold it near and dear to my heart. I think about it often. I'll say this much: I learned a lot about life and being a woman after going through so much. When I found my voice, I attracted a different kind of man. Men prey on women and women prey on men--period.

And at the end of the day, for many, it comes down to how you decide who you are in any given relationship. You have to pay attention, invest your time, and not take yourself too seriously to make a relationship work. I am beginning to appreciate that I'm still learning these lessons; for every smile there is a tear.

A lot of prayer, acknowledgment and acceptance was needed to get here. I blamed myself for a long time for Derrick's death. I would see him in my dreams until one night last week, he came to me and told me that it wasn't my fault and that he isn't mad at me.

He said, "I love you. Move on with your life."

I let it go at that moment, but that won't ever stop me from thinking about all the things I could've done or should have done, although I did the best I could at the time. My silence filled the room like an old sad song, I think about him all the time. He's a spirit that was here for a short time. So that's the story!

"How do you feel now?" Dr. Anirbas asked.

"I feel okay. I'm at a point where I'm not embarrassed to talk about it. It still bothers me, but not like it had in the past. All I can do is go on with life...no one has the power to go back and change the past. I accept the fact that there are some things that I will never understand. I'm sure things happen to everybody. What doesn't kill you is supposed to make you stronger."

"Do you feel like this has made you stronger?" she asked with confidence that it had.

"It did. I learned to lean on my faith a lot more.

Is this the route I would've chosen for myself, *hell no*! But it was the hand that I was dealt. I do understand that my mother was just living her life....

My mother and I can talk now; we can be adults with differences of opinions and points of view of life and respect each other. It took many years, but she finally admitted she was blinded by love and she didn't want to believe that Joe McPherson could ever do a thing like that.

However, to this day, she has never apologized *to anyone*. We were completely dysfunctional both then and now, just not as much. Going through therapy has made me recognize that in order to understand our future, we must first acknowledge our past."

I concluded finally looking into James' eyes.

"Do you feel like you've accomplished that goal, Desiree?" James asked out of the blue.

"Yes and no," I responded honestly to my husband, "I do not feel like I've accomplished that because I lost big when I almost lost you...I lost big when you cheated on me, and you lost big when I cheated on you. I was becoming everything that I hated about my mother; the person I never wanted to be."

My voice became a soft whisper as I continued, "I asked God to give me a life that allowed me to be willing and able to be there for my husband. When you are older and wiser, you are supposed to do better. And that's what I'm doing, trying to be better."

The good doctor allowed my words to sink in before she interjected, "Desiree what is your happy ending?"

"I had a picture of how this was supposed to be, how it was supposed to go, ya know. It's turning out to be nothing like that. I don't think the world truly understands how much your past really shapes who you become, no matter how many times you change your cards. So my happy ending is to simply be happy: happy for my life, my marriage, my family, my career, and most importantly my future."

"So where does this leave you today, right now?" Dr. Anirbas asked particularly interested.

I studied the room and then their faces before I spoke. "I was raised in unfortunate circumstances, that's the truth of the matter. I was raised to be another faceless female in this world, but that is exactly what made me want to fight to stand out. I wanted to stand out and be an example of what was right in a world full of wrong and that set the tone for my life.

I'm not a perfect person and I never claimed to be. The people around me put that pressure on my shoulder and I did my best to carry it...but I cracked under all of the pressure," I said looking at James, "And I think my husband did too. It has always been hard being Desiree Elizabeth and even harder when you add the name Taylor."

James leaned forward in his chair and in the most sincere voice said, "I'm sorry for that...for all of it."

"I know...so am I," I said just as sincerely, "I wanted you here because I wanted you to know that I'm truly ready to move on with our lives. My baggage is mine and it also belongs to James Jones

Taylor as well...the man who promised to love, honor, cherish, and obey until death do us part." I continued looking into James' eyes.

"So for now I sit here with a small swelling in my belly, excited about my future—our future. The three of us, Me, James and Derrick Pender Taylor; It's a boy!" I said with a growing smile while rubbing my lower belly.

James' eyes grew wide as he looked around the room as if he were checking for hidden cameras, "Did you just say what I think you just said?"

I nodded my head in agreement, "Yes."

"I'm having a baby!" He shouted jumping out of his seat, "You're having a boy! I mean we're having a baby boy!" He continued to shout as he got down on his knees in front of me where he embraced me so tightly I could hardly breathe.

"Yes J.J. *we* are having a baby boy!" I said through my laughter.

"But I thought you couldn't have kids from..." he said pausing.

"Well apparently somebody was wrong," I said stroking his face with both of my hands. When I looked over at Dr. Anirbas, she was patting the tears away from her face with a tissue she'd retrieved from her desk.

"Congratulations to both of you," she said sweetly.

"I can't thank you enough for putting my life back together," I said sincerely.

"You had to do the work, and you did Desiree, I'm proud of you. I'm even more excited for your future," she said honestly. "Thank you for allowing me to share in this moment with you."

In the beginning, there was love. In the middle, there was pain. In the end, there is understanding. If this life has taught me anything, it's taught me that I'm a winner for losing and a loser for winning. *It's true*, just take a minute and give it some thought. Sometimes you have to lose to win again. Well I lost and I lost big at an early age, and I made it my business to never lose again.

If love is a battlefield and we all get scars, these were my reminders, my necessary thorns.

If you enjoyed this title, please check out some of my other titles;

- ❖ Those Necessary Thorns: Desiree Elizabeth Taylor

- ❖ Those Necessary Thorns: Sex and Decadence

- ❖ Giggles in the Park

- ❖ Bruised But Not Broken

ABOUT THE AUTHOR

Sabrina Childress is a graduate of Columbia College in Chicago. Sabrina has managed a dual career in public relations as well as the not-for-profit sector through the founding of Position of Pressure nfp, a grassroots domestic violence organization for teens and young adults.

Often described as a paradigm shift, Sabrina writes about struggles, temptations, human nature, and the triumphs of relationships, perceptions, and expectations. As an author, Sabrina likes to challenge others to deal with the real issues of being human.

Follow @TNTBook
Visit www.SabrinaChildress.com

ABOUT ARETHA CEPHUS

Aretha LaSalle Cephus is the loving wife and mother of five children and grandmother to one very special little girl named Makayla. Aretha has been a Certified Nursing Assistant, a Cosmetologist, and is currently owner of "Arielle Unique Salon" located at 4219 Butterfield Road in Hillside, Illinois.

Aretha has always been a very dedicated and hardworking woman; She is the personification of how to succeed when the biggest obstacle gets in the way of your dreams.

***

ACKNOWLEDGMENTS FOR ARETHA CEPHUS

Telling this story has helped me to break down strongholds that have left me incomplete and struggling with the thoughts of what did I do to deserve this? However, through much prayer, I have been able to forgive those who have hurt me, and I hope this book and its lessons will help others do the same... Let go and let God! I especially want to thank my brother who stuck with me through it all. And to my youngest brother who is resting in the arms of God, you will forever be in my heart. R.I.P. Derrick Pender.

P.S.

Sabrina Childress, thanks for the creativity in writing my story.

THOSE NECESSARY THORNS: DERRICK PENDER